THE IRON HORSE

Jenny Hughes

THE IRON HORSE

Copyright: © 2009 by Jenny Hughes
Cover illustration: © Jennifer Bell
Cover layout: Stabenfeldt AS

Typeset by Roberta L. Melzl
Editor: Bobbie Chase
ISBN: 978-1-934983-13-3

Stabenfeldt, Inc.
225 Park Avenue South
New York, NY 10003
www.pony4kids.com

Available exclusively through PONY.

CHAPTER ONE

It started off as a nice, normal day. Well, maybe not *normal*. I'd spent most of it away from my darling pony, Logan, which is pretty unusual, but when we got back home there was no warning of the horror that was to come.

I couldn't wait, of course, even to rush indoors to change, so I leaped out of the car and ran straight to the paddock. Logan, my stunning Andalucian horse, was grazing happily with his pals, seeming completely unconcerned that it had been hours since our morning cuddle. I called his name as I scrambled over the fence and he raised his handsome, iron-gray head and whickered agreeably in return. Khan, my brother's colt, looked up curiously from his usual spot about two feet from Logan's side and watched as I curved my arms around my pony's neck and leaned blissfully against him. The two old ladies of the group, Pearl and Maple, glanced up briefly but seeing no sign of a feed bucket, quickly returned to their grass nibbling.

"We'll have a really good ride tomorrow, baby, a great gallop across the common," I crooned into Logan's ear as I scratched his favorite spot, high on his neck.

"Gemma!" My Mom's voice was mildly annoyed as she called across the field. "Go and change out of that new sweater before it gets ruined!"

"Won't be long." I kissed my pony quickly, gave Khan's shiny black shoulder an affectionate pat, and ran back to the fence.

"Look at you," Mom grumbled good-naturedly. "Covered in hair – couldn't that horse of yours have waited for just a few minutes?"

"I bet Logan wasn't bothered," Craig, my brother, grinned at me. "It's my little sister who's the problem. You can't go a day without him, can you Gem?"

"We miss *each other*," I said with dignity. "You're just jealous because your horse couldn't care less about you."

"How cruel!" He said, pretending my words had stabbed him in the heart. "Maybe if I spent less time studying and more lolling around on the common like you –"

"Lolling! I'll have you know we work hard out there. We –"

"Are you two at it again?" Dad said as he finished unloading the car and thrust a box in Craig's arms. "You're worse than when you were little. Go and put Tessa's cake in the kitchen."

"Cake?" Craig and I looked at one another. "Oh no!"

"You two are rotten," Mom had kicked off her high heels and was padding around barefoot. "Your sister's cooking is coming along nicely."

"Mm," Craig licked a finger and tasted a crumb. "Not up to your standards yet, but good enough for her dork boyfriend, I suppose."

"Behave!" She reached up and pretended to tweak his ear. "Sonny's not a dork."

"You think?" I was in agreement with Craig. "In my

book anyone who likes computers better than animals is definitely a dork."

"*Tessa* likes computers better than animals," Dad joined in the easygoing banter. "Just because you two prefer everything four legged and –"

"Look out, watch your backs – Buster's coming through!" Craig said as he opened the back door.

A small brown and white tornado shot into the kitchen, squealing, whimpering and barking with delight, turning circles and leaping upwards in a frenzy of joy.

"Now here's someone who really *has* missed me," Craig said, letting the little terrier bounce into his arms. "I'm back now, pal, don't worry."

Our other dog Scala, Dad's beautiful collie, pattered quietly into the room and laid her cheek devotedly against Dad's leg. He bent to stroke her and her amber eyes closed with bliss.

"I must say I prefer Scala's greeting," Mom was unloading the dishwasher. "Come on you two, get your old clothes on and sort the menagerie out before I start on supper."

Craig, still being licked to death by his ecstatic terrier, left the kitchen and I ran upstairs to dump the going-out clothes. My usual jeans and T-shirt were on the back of a chair, smelling comfortably and, to me, delightfully of horse and I pulled them on gladly before hurtling back outside.

We're so lucky, my family. Our nice old house stands in a big yard with the wonderful added bonus of three paddocks, two small and one large, plus a small yard of wooden stables my dad built years ago. The stable yard also has a feed and tack room which is only a short distance from the back door so, singing lustily, I zoomed over and quickly prepared four feeds.

Now that the good weather's here our horses live out in the big summer field, so a day away from them, though pretty boring as far as I'm concerned, is easy to manage. Craig and I had checked them all over this morning, making sure the water and the big open-sided shelter was clean, and now all that was needed was a little grooming and a suppertime treat. Maple and Pearl, who do very little work, really didn't need anything with all that yummy grass to eat, but it would feel mean to give them nothing while Logan and Khan snacked away. I picked up my grooming kit and juggled with the four buckets.

"Craig!" I could see him at the back door. "Are you coming?"

"Dad and I are going to take the dogs out," he called back. "You can manage, can't you?"

"Don't you want to see Khan?" I raised my eyebrows at him.

"I've just said hello over the fence. He's fine. I'll give them all a quick look over last thing tonight when I've finished studying."

Craig's in his last year at veterinary college. I know the exams are really hard and it's a heavy workload, but it worried me that he didn't spend enough time with Khan. The horse is only five and there's still a restlessness about him that sometimes spirals into wild behavior.

If Craig put in the hours – I shook my head and got on with my chores. He hadn't had any time to study today, of course, because we'd been at Sonny's parents' home, about 100 miles away. Sonny and our big sister Tessa just got engaged and Mom insisted we all go to meet the family, who I guess will soon be part of *our* family. I can't say the prospect fills me with joy; they're all right, but definitely town people, living in a fancy house on a fancy estate where the only green is an over-manicured park. Sonny's obsessed with stuff like the property market and the latest techno gadgetry and he's never owned so much as a hamster in his life. I always thought Tessa liked the country way we lived. She learned to ride when she was little, clutching Maple's mane just as Craig and I did later, but since she met her boyfriend she's changed. Now all she hankers for is a chic apartment or that trendy must-have, a loft smack in the middle of the city.

I wondered briefly if I'd ever change that much. Tessa's a lot like me in looks – tallish and slim with straight blonde hair which she wears long, while mine's short and spiky. She's super glamorous now but I still think she looks her prettiest when she's messing around in beat up jeans like me. Maybe in a few years I'll be just like her – I grinned as I trundled off with feeds and brushes to the paddock, knowing that I love horses and riding much too deeply to ever become a city girl! The gate into the summer field is at the front so I had to walk down our short driveway to the quiet lane outside before turning right. Dad's always saying he's going to move the gate so we can access it from the yard, but it's one of those things he hasn't gotten around to doing.

Buckets clanging, I quickly unlocked the padlock and closed the gate behind me. Every herd has a hierarchy, an established pecking order, and I allocated the feeds according to that order. Pearl came first, dropping her elegant silvery nose into the sweet chaff mix, then Maple, followed by the boys, Logan and Khan. I'd noticed Khan gets a little nervous feeding out in the open like this, so I stood next to him and rubbed his back comfortingly while he chomped away. Logan, my brave and confident boy, doesn't worry about anything and didn't seem to mind me giving his young friend attention. As usual, I spent much longer than I needed out there in the peaceful, lush paddock, enjoying the final glowing rays of the evening sun and the magical company of my horse family.

As soon as supper was over, Craig and Buster disappeared to put in a few hours' studying while Dad helped me with the last of my homework and Mom dozed comfortably with two of her beloved cats on her lap. It was, as I say, all very normal and unthreatening and as I yawned my way up to bed, looking forward to the next day's ride, I still had no idea what was in store.

"Is that you, Gem?" Craig poked his head out of his room. "Look, I've still got pages to get through – be a doll and do the night check on the paddock, OK?"

"I'll do it from my window," I shook my fist at him. "I'm too tired to go out again."

I'm really lucky that my bedroom looks out to the side of the house and I can see practically the whole of the summer paddock. If the horses are over this way I can see them, even at night. The lights from the house outline each horse as they contentedly wander across the grass. I threw the window open and leaned out, breathing in the soft summer air. No, I was out of luck, they were either on the far side of the field or, unlikely on such a calm, nice evening, out of sight inside their shelter. Sighing deeply I wandered back out, giving Craig's door an annoyed thump as I passed.

"I can't see them. I've got to go out."

He muttered something in reply but didn't leap up to do it for me. I could hear my parents talking quietly, easily in the living room as I went by and smiled as Scala gave the low "yip" that meant she'd heard me open the back door. Taking a flashlight and pushing my feet into the nearest boots I ambled outside and walked across to the paddock fence. Light streamed out with me, illuminating the post and rails and a wide expanse of field behind it. I scanned the far stretches of grass wearily, eyes straining to see a familiar shape looming out of the dark. It was very quiet. There were small rustlings in the hedge to my right and high in a beech tree an owl hooted.

"Logan?" I didn't yell as I didn't want to disturb his sleep if he was resting somewhere in the unlit stretch of paddock, but when still no gentle answering whicker came, I raised my voice. "Logan! Come on, baby, where are you?"

He *always* responded to my call, not at a mad, flat-out canter or anything, but he loves to say hello whatever time it is. Faintly worried now, I clambered over the top bar of the fence and plodded across the brightly lit strip of grass, turning on the flashlight as I did so. Its powerful beam cut through the velvet blackness ahead, picking up two flashes of white as feeding rabbits scuttled away, tufty tails bobbing. I kept walking, sweeping the flashlight beam to cover every corner of the field and now I was calling urgently, "Logan! Logan!"

11

There was only the shelter to check but when the bright searchlight played inside, it showed an empty interior, the floor still swept clean and bare.

"Maybe, just maybe they're sleeping behind it." I'd started to run, panic rising in my throat.

I was willing the four horses to be there, trying to convince myself that as I rounded the shelter's side eight dark, beautiful eyes would blink sleepily back at me. But there was nothing. Another scuffling of rabbits, another hoot from the night owl and I was running back to the house, boots flapping awkwardly, my face wet with tears of sheer panic.

"Mom! Dad!" I hurtled into the house, my voice rising to a scream. "They've been stolen! Quick, call the police – the horses –"

Dad ran into the hall and I threw myself into his arms, sobbing and shaking.

"Shh, Gemma, it's OK, calm down," he hugged me close, patting my back soothingly. "Take a deep breath and tell us what's happened."

"The – the –" I swallowed convulsively. "The horses are gone. All of them."

With a great clattering rush Craig reached the foot of the stairs, followed closely by Buster. "Did you say stolen? You saw someone stealing our horses?"

"Yes. No," I tried to pull myself together. "I didn't see anything, but the field is empty. I looked everywhere and then I ran –"

"Come on," Dad sprang into action. "Get your shoes on, Craig, and grab the head collars. If the fence is broken they might have just wandered off."

Mom ran to grab more flashlights while I kicked off the oversized boots and found my own.

"You stay here with me, Gemma," Mom said, her face dead white. "If we need to call the police –"

"I can't," I said. I'd stopped crying but I was still shaking. "I have to go too, I have to find them."

Craig and I were faster than Dad, running along the drive and turning right onto the dark, quiet lane outside. The field gate, when we reached it, was wide open, the chain and padlock lying uselessly on the grass verge.

"They must have cut through it," I shone my flashlight desperately around us while Craig picked up the padlock and studied it.

"No," he said slowly. "It hasn't been cut. It looks as though it wasn't locked properly."

"What?" I grabbed it out of his hand. "I always lock it! I shut the gate, put the empty buckets on the ground, then fixed the chain and spun the padlock code numbers. Look, you can see I did!"

Dad, panting slightly, peered over my shoulder. "Can you remember the lock clicking into place? I noticed it's pretty stiff sometimes."

"Yes. No." I shook my head, trying to clear the panic that was clogging my brain. "I can't remember. Are you saying it was *my* fault our horses have been stolen, Dad?"

"Just calm down, Gemma," he said, shining his flashlight on the ground. "Thieves use transport, a horse trailer, and Scala would have heard that and barked. There aren't any tire tracks anyway, but look at this." His light was trained on a slick of dried mud on the road. "Fresh looking hoofprints from an unshod horse."

"Only Maple doesn't have shoes," I said, trying to make sense of it. "And she hasn't been outside the field today."

"I think," Dad looked ghostly in the spooky flashlight light, "that somehow the gate opened and the horses have just gotten loose."

"In which case they're somewhere in the lane," Craig said, shining his beam as far as he could. "Where would they go? In the direction of the common, I guess."

The huge rush of relief I was feeling was extinguished as a new fear clutched at me.

"If they went the other way they're heading for the road!"

The lane where we live is a really quiet one, ending just beyond our house with a big stretch of open common land so there's no through traffic to worry about, but away to the right, about a mile or so, the other end meets the main road into the nearby town of Brigham. None of us said it out loud but we all knew our beloved horses stood little chance of survival if they ran out into the heavy, fast moving mass of cars and trucks on Brigham Road.

"Gemma," Dad's voice was amazingly calm, "Logan always responds to your voice, doesn't he? Start walking and call his name – try to sound as normal as you can."

"Which way should I go?" I'd have to really fight to keep any note of panic out of my voice.

He hesitated. "We'll head toward the road while Craig checks out the common."

I nodded and walked with him, our flashlights forming a wide pool of light in the inky darkness of the lane.

"Logan!" There was a distinct tremor when I tried the first time but I stamped it down fiercely. "Logan, come on baby!"

We'd only gone a few hundred yards when I stopped and gripped Dad's arm. "Listen!"

He stood stock-still and shook his head doubtfully. "I can't hear –"

The answering whinny was louder now and I felt my heart soar like a bird.

"You're right!" he said and we ran swiftly in the direction of the wonderful sound, through an open gateway on the opposite side of the lane.

Again I was quicker, racing along the paved stretch of drive till suddenly the scene exploded into brightness – I'd triggered some security lighting. The extensively planted front yard was now bathed in neon and it was all I could do to stop from bursting into near-hysterical laughter. Walking toward me across a once perfect stretch of lawn was Logan, his gorgeous dark eyes glowing. Behind him Khan stood hock deep in the middle of a flowerbed and ahead was the stately silver bulk of Pearl as she leaned over to pull at the leaves of an ornately planted urn.

"Oh *Logan*!" I stepped forward and buried my face in his neck.

"What the –" With a crash the front door of the house flew open and a disheveled figure in a bathrobe stared at us all in horror. "What are you doing with those creatures on my – oh no!"

Pearl, reaching for something particularly tasty, had sent the urn crashing.

"I'm so sorry, Bryan," Dad moved quickly over to slip a head collar on his horse. "I don't know how they got out, but of course I'll pay for any damage."

I buckled Logan's strap and slid a rope around Khan's neck. He, naughty boy, was obviously enjoying himself where he was and took some persuading to move but I finally managed. Bryan Edwards, the house's owner, was running madly around, picking up bits of discarded flowers and moaning loudly while Dad tried to placate him. I quickly finished checking every corner of the once pristine front garden bed.

"Excuse me," I had to call out twice. "Sorry, Mr. Edwards, but is there a way through to the back?"

"What?" he straightened up from patting a clod of turf back in place. "Don't you think you've caused enough trouble out here?"

"Yes, I'm sorry but –" I took one last look around. "There's still one horse missing. Dad, Maple's not here. Could she have gone into the backyard?"

"No she could not. The gate is kept securely locked and bolted – oh, just look at my roses!"

"We're truly sorry," Dad said. He led Pearl onto the driveway and took Khan from me. "Gemma, you and Logan go and see if you can find Maple while I try to calm things down here."

As I hurried back out to the lane I could still hear Bryan Edwards' voice getting higher and higher with every complaint. For a few minutes I walked with my arms wrapped tight around my pony, telling him over and over again how much I loved him and how terrified I'd been.

"I don't know how it happened and I'm really sorry if it was my fault," I gave him one more kiss and shone the flashlight around us, "but the first thing we have to do is find Maple. She can't be far, can she?"

I was sure we'd find the elderly bay pony a little further down the lane, maybe quietly cropping grass on the side of the road. I really, really hoped she wasn't in yet another garden – at this rate we'd have the whole street on our backs – but when I passed the next three houses with no sight or sound of little Maple, the great knot of fear had formed inside me again. The thought of the lethal Brigham Road kept pounding at my brain, bringing with it the by now familiar wave of sheer, utter terror.

CHAPTER TWO

Ahead of us the lane was brighter, illuminated by lamps in the gateways of the next few houses, so I decided the higher viewpoint from Logan's back would be an advantage in my search. Vaulting aboard I peered anxiously over hedges and fences, hoping against hope that I'd see the compact shape of our missing pony. The gates I passed now were firmly closed and the lane curved, quiet and deserted around the next corner. As we rounded the bend Logan pricked his intelligent ears and my heart thumped against my ribs but to my disappointment it was a person, not a pony, he'd spotted. Someone was slouching against a wall further along and I saw him take a swig from a can as his head swiveled in my direction.

"Hey, guys, get a load of this!"

Two more youths slid down from the top of the wall and for a moment I hesitated, but then pushed Logan onward.

"Hello," I sounded silly even to me. "I don't suppose you've seen a pony come this way, have you?"

"No," the first one said, his blond hair shaved so close it made him look somehow menacing. He gave me an unpleasant sneer. "It's a little careless of you to lose one, isn't it sweetheart?"

"She got out of her field," I felt my lower lip tremble. "She's probably scared and –"

"Oh dear, what a shame," Blondie stood up and crushed his empty can macho fashion, making Logan flinch.

"Don't be a moron, Vinny." A tall, dark figure appeared from out of the blackness. "Sorry, we didn't mean to scare your horse. If we see the one missing we'll let you know."

"Thank you," I shortened the lead rope, my makeshift "reins," and moved Logan forward again, keeping a wary eye on the blond Vinny.

He sneered up at me but stayed quiet, and the dark-haired one met my eyes.

There was something in his look that made me say, "If you find her, just put your arm around her neck and she'll follow you. We live in the end house, Green Acres."

The other three sniggered but he nodded gravely, "OK."

I rode past, my heart hammering so loudly I was sure they could hear it. Another house, another locked gate and my desperation was becoming more intense. I could now hear the menacing drone of traffic ahead and knew we were less than a quarter of a mile from the junction with Brigham Road. We'd entered a pool of darkness again, my flashlight cutting through it like a beacon as I shone it from side to side. Logan, bless him, was being amazing, bravely doing everything I asked without hesitation despite what must seem to him a really weird situation. I patted him lovingly, bending close to tell him how wonderful he was – and he stopped dead in his tracks.

"It's all right," I squeezed his sides encouragingly. "I know it's scary out here but we have to find her, so walk on, Logan."

He took one step and stopped again, his eyes glowing red in the flashlight light, his ears flicking back and forth. I sat very, very still, listening intently with him. The smallest sound reached my ears, probably a mouse or a bat, but Logan's nostrils flared and he gave the soft whicker that meant recognition. There was no mistaking the response, a shrill whinny, which I knew, despite its high note of fear, was Maple's.

"You found her!" I slid from my pony's back and shone the flashlight ahead.

An impenetrable looking hedge bordered the side of the lane, stretching both ways in an uninterrupted line. Maple called again, more urgently and most definitely from somewhere behind it. I spoke her name, trying to sound calm and in control.

"It's OK, Maple, we're here. Come this way, follow my voice, there's a good girl."

She whinnied again, her distress patently clear.

"She must be trapped," I said and pushed uselessly against the thick growth of the hedge. "She's inside someone's grounds. We'll have to find the gate, Logan, come on."

"It's way down there." The tall guy I'd just spoken to appeared silently at our side, his dark good looks profiled in the light of my flashlight. "And all locked up. You won't get in."

"Maple, our pony, she's in there," I looked again into the same dark eyes. "She sounds as though she's stuck somehow."

"This way," he turned and quickly walked several yards to our right.

20

The line of hedge looked exactly the same but he shoved against it with his shoulder and it gave way easily. Quickly, I tied Logan's lead rope to a branch and followed the tall figure inside. He moved easily through a dense strip of wood, stopping abruptly as the trees thinned.

"There she is."

The beam of my flashlight shone brightly, wonderfully on Maple's small, blunt head and she called again but didn't move.

"There's something wrong," I said, wanting to run to her although I knew I mustn't make her panic. "Oh no, she's caught in some wire!"

Trembling I knelt beside the old pony, trying to stroke her comfortingly while examining her off fore hoof. A trail of thin, vicious-looking wire had snagged around the lower leg, wrapping itself around the pastern.

"We'll need wire-cutters. I'll have to go and get Dad or Craig," I said. I stood up and Maple tried to move with me.

"By the time you fetch anyone she'll have ripped that foot to pieces. Let me have a look."

He crouched down to inspect the damage and I said stupidly, "I don't even know your name."

"Jason," he said briefly. "I've only got a penknife, but if I saw through this end of the wire, the other end will be free. We can get her moving without the wire tightening any more."

As if to illustrate his point, Maple tried to lift her foot and I saw the wire dig deeper. Jason dug around in his pocket for the knife and set to work right away. It was spooky and surreal, the three of us pressed together in a pool of light in the deep velvet blackness of this unknown garden.

"You see," Jason's long finger traced the wire. "This length's connected to that post over there and Maple walked into the broken end, so it got wrapped around her foot. There's no way I can untangle it but if I can manage to snap this end free she should be able to walk."

He bent his dark head and started sawing away, pressing as closely as he could to the pony's leg. Every so often he'd straighten up and stroke her, his voice and hands very gentle. Maple seemed to trust him completely, even dropping her nose to rest on his shoulder, finding comfort in his calm presence.

"She likes you," I remarked, still feeling quite emotional. "You're obviously good with horses."

"Thanks." The upward flash from his eyes was warm. "This is actually the nearest I've ever been to one."

I was genuinely amazed and opened my mouth to say so when he growled softly. "What's the matter?" I steadied the flashlight and peered down. "Oh, there's blood on your hands."

"Don't worry, it's mine not Maple's. Phew, that's it – I cut through the wire." He stood up, still keeping his movements smooth, and as he stroked the pony's neck I could see the blood still trickling from the cut on his hand.

Maple took a hesitant step, obviously feeling the grip of the wire still wound around her pastern but when it didn't dig deeper she gained confidence and walked quickly beside me. We retraced our route through the narrow belt of trees and Jason parted the gap in the hedge to allow us through. Logan, waiting patiently in the dark lane, gave his lovely whicker of greeting and the two ponies touched noses in an affectionate gesture that made Jason smile. The smile altered his face completely, lifting its dark, moody lines into something that took me by surprise.

"OK," he said, obviously not noticing the effect he'd had on me. "Do you think she can walk as far as your house or – hold on, someone's coming."

Even before I heard him panting I knew it was my dad lumbering toward us behind his flashlight.

"You found her! Oh, well *done*, Gemma!"

"It was thanks to Jason here," I said, rapidly explaining about the wire.

"Wonderful, wonderful," Dad said as he grabbed Jason's hand and shook it enthusiastically. "I can't thank you enough."

"It's OK. I hope Maple's leg is all right. See you around."

Before I could say anything he turned away into the darkness and vanished.

Dad, after examining Maple's leg, decided we shouldn't risk walking her any further. "Send Craig up here with some wire cutters," he told me. "You and Logan can reach him a lot quicker than I can."

I vaulted onto my pony's back and urged her toward the house. Cantering on the grass we quickly passed the lamp-lit section of the lane and I was relieved to see that Vinny and his two pals had gone. Craig was at the field gate fiddling with the padlock. When I gave him a brief outline he grabbed some cutters from the toolbox he was using and took off immediately.

"The lock's working OK now," he yelled back, "so we put Khan and Pearl back in there."

Although I knew this was a perfectly sensible thing to do I was reluctant to simply open the gate and turn Logan out again. Instead I rode him down the driveway into the yard at the back of the house, justifying my actions by telling myself I wanted to check him out thoroughly in the bright light of his stable. Mom came out immediately and helped me put a bed down.

"He'd be safe in the field you know," she said, giving us both a hug. "Dad thinks it was some kind of freak accident that they got out – it's never happened before in the twenty years we've been here so you shouldn't worry about it happening again."

"Yeah I know, but –" I started, suddenly feeling shaky again. "Oh, it was horrible, Mom, first thinking they'd been stolen, then worrying that Maple had gotten as far as Brigham Road and –"

She hugged me even harder. "You're in shock. You check that boy of yours over and settle him down wherever you feel happiest."

While I carefully examined every beautiful iron-gray inch of Logan she listened to Maple's story and quickly made a warm mash for the two horses to comfort them after what had been a pretty scary adventure. She brought it over just as Dad, Craig and Maple returned wearily to the yard. Craig had carefully cut away the short length of wire left around the pony's lower leg, and thought there was no real harm done.

"There's an indentation but the wire hasn't broken the skin," he said, checking again under the stable light. "We'll keep her in tonight and look at it again in the morning. That new boyfriend of yours did a good job, Gemma."

"He's not my boyfriend," I replied, knowing he was

teasing. "But yes – I don't know what I would have done without Jason."

"Jason eh?" He whistled and ruffled my hair. "He must have moved in recently, but I can see from your face he's going to be the new man in your life."

"Don't be stupid," I objected, secretly *loving* the idea. "I'll probably never see him again."

To my delight, however, I was completely wrong about that. The next morning, being Sunday, we were able to spend plenty of time with the horses. Craig, in his nearly-a-vet mode, got me trotting on Maple to make sure she was completely sound and pronounced her one hundred percent, so we were able to put her and Logan back in the summer paddock with their friends. It was a beautiful spring day with a gentle breeze stirring the blossom on the trees while the sun glimmered through their newly green leaves. I lay in the grass watching Logan and Khan indulge in a lengthy session of mutual grooming while Maple, seeming none the worse for her nocturnal wanderings, grazed contentedly alongside Pearl. It was a happy, peaceful scene, as far removed from the nightmare of last night's panic-fueled horror as you can get, and I just couldn't stop smiling.

"Maple looks fine, doesn't she?" He was at the gate, sitting on the bike he'd leaned against it.

"Oh, hi, Jason," I said and scrambled to my feet, wishing hard I'd put on something more flattering than the baggy old T shirt I was wearing. "Come and see her so she can say thank you."

He hesitated. "Um – don't worry – I just wanted to make sure she was OK."

25

Maple, hearing his voice, lifted her head and to my surprise gave a pleased whinny.

"Oh come on," I said, grinning at him. "You can't ignore that. She really wants to see you."

"OK," he said, lying the bike down. "I'll climb over, OK?"

As he walked toward us he looked, I found myself thinking, even better in the daylight. His dark eyes, though slightly watchful, were warm and when Maple pushed her nose affectionately against him the fabulous smile again transformed his face. He spent a long time petting the old pony till she decided she'd had enough and wandered off to continue her grazing. Showing off a little, I pointed out how Logan was still leaning against me in complete bliss as I scratched his neck and gently pulled his velvet ears.

"That black one hasn't gone far either," he stretched a hand and stroked Khan's shoulder.

Khan, always a little nervous, hung back but Jason, using the calm, soothing tone I knew, gradually got the horse to come nearer and nearer.

"You really are a natural." I'd never seen Khan so relaxed. "I can't believe you've never had anything to do with horses before."

"Totally true," he said and smiled again as Khan blew curiously into his face. "I've always thought they were beautiful animals but –"

"You must be Jason," Craig said, appearing suddenly at the gate. I was completely unprepared for his aggressive attitude. "So how come you were hanging out on our street last night? I've been asking around – you're not from around here, are you?"

Jason dropped the hand that was stroking Khan. "No."

"Hey!" I said, really annoyed at my brother's tone. "*Jason,* if you remember, is the guy who rescued Maple. This is Craig. You'll have to excuse his manners. He doesn't appear to have any."

"I just came from Bryan Edwards' place," Craig said, vaulting into the field. "He's big and chunky, like Dad and in a belligerent mood he looks pretty threatening. He's still putting Dad through the wringer about the damage the horses did to his garden. Oh, and his theory is that they were deliberately let out of the paddock by a gang of kids from Brigham. Is that where you're from, Jason?"

"Yeah, I'm from the town, but as far as I know *your* street is a public road," Jason retaliated, not looking even remotely scared of him. "So why do I need a reason to be here?"

They were squaring up to each other like a couple of prizefighters and I opened my mouth to tell Craig to stop.

"Point taken," my brother looked really mean. "But for a start there's nothing for you to *do* on our street and it seems an odd coincidence that our field gate should mysteriously open at the same time you were around, doesn't it?"

"Look," Jason's fists were clenched. "If you're saying I'm the one who let them out – well OK, I might not know much about horses, but I do know they don't mix well with traffic."

"Like that would bother you! Bryan says he chased your group off earlier. Was that when you decided to unlatch our gate?"

"You heard what I said. There's no way I'd ever, *ever* risk hurting an animal like that. I swear I didn't touch your stupid gate!" There was the genuine, unmistakable ring of truth in his voice and I stepped forward, eyes blazing at Craig.

"Look at his hands! They were *bleeding* last night when he was trying to cut Maple free! How can you possibly think *Jason* –"

"We don't," My dad's calm voice came as a huge relief. "Of course we don't, Jason. I can tell immediately what kind of person you are and I apologize for my son's behavior. I think even *he* can now see you're telling the truth."

Craig, his belligerent stance suddenly sagging, dropped his hard gaze. "Sorry. I thought it was too much of a coincidence, your gang being here and our horses getting out. I guess I just jumped to the wrong conclusion."

"If you're going to yell at anyone, have a go at me," I said, still furious. "I'm the idiot who didn't put the lock on properly so maybe I messed up the latch as well."

"No one is doling out blame here," Dad said firmly. "Despite Bryan Edwards' somewhat wild assumptions I'm still sure the whole episode was an accident. Once his garden's back to its former glory Bryan will calm down. There was no other harm done so let's just forget the whole thing and move on."

"I suppose you're right," Craig said, but he still didn't look totally convinced, I thought. "OK, sorry Jason."

He reluctantly put out his hand and Jason, equally reluctant, shook it.

"Come on," I said, wanting to defuse the situation. I put a head collar on my pony. "I'm going to lunge Logan for ten minutes or so. Will you give me a hand, Jason?"

"Sure. Uh –" he shrugged helplessly and lowered his voice, "except I don't actually know how."

"Oh Gem," Craig turned back from the gate. "I'm miles behind with my studying. You wouldn't do me a favor and give Khan a session too?"

"OK," I handed the black pony's head collar to Jason, very matter-of-factly. "Bring your new friend with you, please."

He watched me fasten Logan's buckle and copied what I'd done, bringing Khan into line behind me. Acting very cool and cheerful, I led the way out of the field, determined to make Jason feel glad he'd come back to see us. Although I was mad at the way Craig had gone after him, I couldn't help the nagging feeling that my brother had a point. It *did* seem strange that Vinny and the rest of them had spent the evening hanging around a dark, and to them, totally boring country lane and I couldn't help noticing that Jason had side-stepped the issue pretty neatly. I was totally convinced he'd been telling the truth about the horses though, and as far as I was concerned he was someone I definitely wanted to get to know better. If that meant delaying the questions and doing what my dad had called "moving on," I was all for it – in a big, big way.

29

CHAPTER THREE

"So what exactly is *this* for?" Jason, gently stroking Khan's nose, watched as I stood in the center of the ring with Logan on the lunge rein. Holding the rein in my left hand with the slack carefully coiled, I directed my pony in a counter-clockwise circle around me.

"It has lots of uses but today I'm doing it because I want to look at his movement. He seems absolutely fine after last night but I want to make sure he isn't stiff or sore before I ride him."

"And you'll do the same for Khan when you've finished?" Jason seemed genuinely interested.

"Same routine," I put Logan smoothly into trot. "But in his case it's for a different reason. Craig probably won't have time to ride today. Listening to Bryan Edwards ranting used up too much of his study time, but this way at least Khan gets some exercise and a little training."

"I see," he said, and he smiled as the black pony nuzzled his arm. "Though personally I think your brother's nuts."

I frowned, feeling a little worried. "Because of the way he accused you? He *did* say sorry when he realized –"

"Yeah right," he said cryptically, "I just meant – well if *I* could ride, nothing would keep me from taking this beautiful horse out."

Still concentrating on lunging, I flashed him a quick smile. "Maybe you should learn then."

"I can't afford lessons," he said simply. "They cost a fortune, don't they?"

"Well, you should try Green Acres School of Riding," Dad said, walking up quietly behind him. "We have very reasonable rates for people who rescue our horses, you know, and Gemma's a pretty good teacher."

I brought Logan to an obedient halt and looked across at both of them.

Jason, his long fingers still stroking the black pony, looked – well – stunned.

"That would be fantastic! How much would it cost?"

Dad laughed, making Khan toss his head nervously. "You can help with the chores as payment. My daughter's always moaning she has to do everything herself."

"That's right," I joined in, keeping it carefully casual. "Some grooming and mucking out would easily cover a lesson, I think."

"No!" His face, lit up, was incredible. "You mean I could ride Khan?"

"Uh – he's a little young and wild for a beginner," Dad said tactfully. "I was thinking of Pearl. She could use a little more exercise."

"Wow," Jason went pale with excitement. "I could come over every day and help with the work."

"What about school?" I blurted out. "You're only about fourteen, same as me, aren't you?"

"Yeah, more or less – I'll be fifteen in a few months." He seemed unsure of my reaction and the light faded from his eyes. "I meant every morning before school or whatever, but if you don't want to be bothered it doesn't matter."

"Sure I do!" I forgot about sounding cool. "I'd *love* to teach you. Riding is the best thing in the world."

"Then it's settled," Dad said, and he watched, approving as Jason soothed the high-strung Khan. "It's the least we can do after last night."

And, I thought silently, *it'll make up for Craig throwing wild accusations around. Dad – you're brilliant!*

Once I'd finished lunging Logan I put him in his stable, pleased with the way he'd worked and the effortless, free flowing rhythm of his movement. I showed Jason how to adjust the cavesson to fit Khan and tried not to notice how close we were standing as I started moving the black horse forward.

"Khan's got a low boredom threshold," I explained, "so once he's warmed up I'll vary the direction and his paces to keep him interested."

I always think lunging, though interesting to do, is pretty dull to watch, but Jason seemed riveted, studying Khan intently and asking endless questions about the technique. I worked the pony intensely for about twenty-five minutes, then brought him to halt and praised him. Jason joined in that part with enthusiasm and I was surprised to see how the usually undemonstrative horse responded to him.

"OK," I smiled at him. "We'll take Khan back to the field and bring Pearl out if you like."

He stood very still. "You mean I can ride her now?"

"Sure, if you want," I said, working hard at making it seem like no big deal, afraid he might back out if I pushed too hard. "I'll show you how to tack her up, then you can sit on her and see how it feels."

"Fantastic!" His eyes, often wary and hooded, shone with an intense glow.

He led Khan back along the driveway, walking him level with his left shoulder as I'd shown him. I watched him gently release the pony into the paddock, crooning quietly to the youngster the whole time. He struggled slightly with Pearl's battered old head collar, trying to put it on inside out on his first attempt, but he soon sorted it out and Pearl followed him agreeably, obviously liking his voice and manner. I showed him how to brush the gray mare, pick out her hooves and make sure her bridle and saddle were fitted correctly and comfortably. Then I led the way back to the ring. I think by then I was more nervous than Jason and found myself fervently praying that his sudden, unexpected introduction to the joys of riding wouldn't be a total anti-climax.

Pearl, who's over twenty and quite staid nowadays, is a big horse, well over 16 hands high, and it takes a lot of effort for even an experienced rider to spring lightly into her saddle. I described the process a few times, demonstrated it once, then held Pearl's head as Jason placed his left hand in front of her withers and, steadying the stirrup with his right hand, got his left foot into the iron. Pivoting his body, he moved his right hand to the far side of the saddle and straightened both knees. Instead of the smooth, upward thrust he was aiming for there was an ungainly flailing of arms and legs as he floundered around helplessly.

"You need more spring," I offered encouragingly, "so

that when you're level with Pearl's back you can swing your right leg over without touching her quarters."

Jason groaned, patted Pearl apologetically and untangled himself.

"Don't worry," I said hastily. "I'll go grab a box – you can use it as a mounting block."

"No," he positioned himself correctly, his left side against Pearl's near shoulder, and gathered his reins as I'd shown him.

Muttering the sequence of moves under his breath, he tried again, with more upward movement this time, and very nearly made it.

"I'm not hurting her, am I?" Back on the ground again he looked at the stoic horse anxiously.

"She's fine," I reassured him. "Let me get that box now."

"No, let me try just one more time." This time he gave it everything he had, even remembering to lower himself quietly into the saddle once his right leg had cleared her back.

"Well *done*," I congratulated him. I stood back and eyed him critically, adjusting the length of the stirrups leathers a notch. "Now, I'm just going to lead you around the ring and I want you to sit comfortably and naturally – if it looks wrong we'll straighten it out in a minute."

To my relief he didn't wriggle around or fuss with his hands and after one circuit I again stood back and evaluated his position.

"That's really good," I praised, somehow not surprised. "Your balance and your lower leg position look nearly perfect. Try to keep your elbows close to your sides, but they must remain supple and loose to allow correct hand movement."

"Hands are really important, aren't they?" he said. "I've heard people talk about top riders having good hands."

"They're vital," I nodded, mentally drawing a straight line to pass through his ear, shoulder, hip and back of heel. "And you're holding them correctly, thumbs uppermost and backs facing directly outwards."

"It feels fabulous," he said. The smile that made my insides melt was back on his face. "Am I the one making Pearl move? She's still going even though you're not leading her now."

"She's a very well-schooled lady," I said and grinned up at him. "She's obeying my voice. I told her to walk on and that's what she's doing, but it won't be long before you learn the aids you need to give her."

We spent nearly an hour in the ring, and I've never seen anyone work harder. He seemed to enjoy every minute, though, and when I finally called a halt his disappointment was very apparent.

"You did great." I watched him remove the helmet Dad had loaned him and resisted the urge to run my fingers through his gorgeous thick hair. "You'll probably feel a little stiff and sore tomorrow but –"

"Can I come over after school?" His voice was eager. "And I can ride my bike over first thing if you need a hand in the morning."

"There's no need. Summer mornings are easy," I told him, massaging Pearl's back as he removed her saddle. "But yeah, you can have another lesson about 4 o'clock if you like."

"Oh I definitely like," he copied what I was doing. "That's if it won't tire Pearl too much."

"Like Dad said, she could use a bit of exercise. She's starting to get fat." I stood back and watched him. "An hour or so of walk and trot will do her good."

Even after he'd taken Pearl back to the field, Jason seemed in no hurry to leave but I wanted to take Logan out for our promised ride across the common.

"You can stay if you like," I smiled as he tore himself away from Khan with an obvious effort.

"No, I'd better go. Your family will think I've moved in!" He grinned at me and I marveled again at the difference it made to his face. "You're sure they'll be all right with me turning up again tomorrow?"

"Absolutely," I said firmly, deciding I'd soon sort Craig out if he objected. "I was thinking, we've got some books indoors, basic equitation and so on. You can borrow a couple if you like."

"Yes, please," he followed me to the house, waiting outside while I ran in and grabbed the books.

"You can come in, you know," I pulled on my riding boots. "Mom will make you a drink and –"

"Thanks, but I've got to go," he wheeled his bike up the drive, tucking the books carefully into his sweatshirt.

He didn't look back or wave or anything but I still felt elated and sort of squirmy as I picked up my tack and went into Logan's stable.

"I know it's the riding that's bringing him back tomorrow," I whispered in my pony's silky ear as I adjusted his bridle, "but he must like me a bit, don't you think?"

Logan blew solemnly down his nose which I felt sure

meant he agreed. He was looking forward to going out, stepping smartly from his stable to walk briskly along the drive. The other horses looked up briefly, then returned to their grazing as we turned left, away from their field. It's only a short ride to the common and we hardly ever see a car. I love the freedom of riding my pony along the quiet, leafy lane and always enjoy myself immensely but today had even more sparkle and I sang, loud and unmelodious, as we reached the broad turning circle at the end of the road.

The common is well fenced, with a "horses and walkers only" type of gate to maneuver and I was still singing as Logan made his way neatly though it. The expanse of common land lay peaceful and inviting under the warm spring sun, stretching ahead in a gloriously wild landscape of burgeoning color.

Once Logan was properly warmed up we cantered to the summit of our favorite hill, along a softly undulating path ahead with scrubby grass and a few delicate patches of wildflowers. A small copse grew on the hill, filled with birdsong and fingers of light as the sun's rays dappled the earth beneath the trees. Then we went through a stream, Logan's dark gray legs looking almost black as he surged strongly through the water, up a bank and over a fallen tree, a superb jump by my clever horse. Another good canter, longer this time, the path snaking its way between bracken, fern and briar. With a perfect flying leg change we were heading toward a broad track of springy turf, perfect for galloping. It was glorious, heady excitement and I loved every moment, reveling as always in the sensation of power and speed and the warm feeling of being one with Logan.

"You," I gave my pony a long rein so he could stretch his neck muscles in a cooling down walk, "are the most wonderful boy in the world, and sharing this feeling with Jason one day will be so perfect I'll – I'll –" The thought was so exhilarating, the surge of happiness so strong, I burst into song again.

Logan flicked an ear and shook his head, making me laugh which at least stopped my singing – probably a great relief to my horse and any nearby wildlife! We stayed out for another hour or so, thoroughly enjoying ourselves and only started heading for home when hunger pangs reminded me I needed some food.

I knew my family was spending the day at home and wasn't expecting any visitors so I was surprised to see a big, swanky car parked outside our front door. Selfishly hoping it didn't mean eating was going to be delayed, I rode straight into the yard, sorted out my pony and led him back to the paddock. I shut the gate firmly and shook it to make sure the heavy latch was in place, and then checked the padlock three times. It was much easier to lock since Craig had fixed it last night but I knew I'd feel uneasy every time I walked away from it. As I sauntered back to the house I wondered about buying a second lock, a sort of double insurance, so I'd always know I'd secured the gate properly.

"Gemma!" It was Craig's voice and he sounded annoyed again.

"I'm coming," I heard the surly note in my own voice and told myself my brother was in big trouble if he was going to rant on about Jason again. "What do you want?"

Glancing behind him he stepped outside to meet me.

"More trouble," he said quietly. "Another neighbor's come over to complain about last night and you know how upset Dad gets."

"Who is it?" I definitely didn't recognize the car.

"New guy, moved in a month or two ago in that big house at the top end of the lane – the one where you found Maple. His name's Brad Tomas and he's –"

"Gemma – there you are!" Dad sounded beleaguered. "Mr. – uh – Tomas would like a word."

Sighing inwardly, I kicked off my boots and went in the front door as opposed to my usual route at the back. Brad Tomas was waiting in the first room off the hall, a pleasantly shabby place where Dad does his work.

"Please," Dad hurried in before me. "Do take a seat."

"As I said, I prefer to stand," he was tall and thin with a slightly pinched face and a clipped way of speaking. "So, Gemma, your father tells me you were trespassing last night."

"That's not what I said," the frown lines between Dad's eyebrows were deeper than I'd ever seen. "Bryan Edwards told Mr. Tomas about our horses, Gemma, and – um –"

"I discovered hoofprints in my garden this morning," the man cut in. "And as my gates were firmly locked I could only imagine a break-in of some sort. I've found evidence before, someone entering my grounds during the hours of darkness, and this time there seems to be a clear indication of who it is."

"Well it was definitely me last night," I looked him directly in the eye. "But it was an emergency. If I could, I'd have asked your permission to get Maple but there wasn't time."

"Maple?" He spoke the word with distaste.

"The oldest of our horses," Dad broke in. "I tried to tell you –"

"I'd prefer to hear what your daughter has to say, seeing she was the one who illegally entered my premises."

"Actually it was Maple who did the entering," I didn't like his manner. "I just – followed."

"The pony was trapped you see, her leg caught in wire –" Poor Dad was trying to make up for the fact I wasn't being apologetic.

Brad Tomas held up a hand to stop him. "So there you were – uh, Gemma – outside in the pitch black lane, yet you knew your animal was inside my grounds – how?"

"I heard her," I said. "At least Logan, my pony, heard her. We couldn't see a thing, just that tall, thick hedge of yours but Maple called to Logan and I could tell she was in some sort of trouble."

"How?" His eyes narrowed so much they practically disappeared.

"Because of the way she sounded," I said impatiently. "You don't know anything about horses, do you?"

"I know they shouldn't be inside my grounds in the middle of the night," he snapped.

"Yeah," I shot a quick glance at Dad. "Sorry about that, but it was a complete accident. We don't know exactly what happened but they've never gotten out before and it was so horrible we'll make sure they never do it again."

He made the irritating hand gesture again. "That side of it is *your* problem, frankly, but I still fail to understand how your horse got inside my grounds, whether by accident or not. The gates were firmly locked and, as you mentioned, the hedge around the perimeter is completely impenetrable."

There was a short, pregnant pause.

"Um," I said. "Well, it's not, actually. There's one part that's sort of loose. It looks the same as the rest but Maple must have pushed up against it and it just gave way."

"What?" His eyes vanished again. "I checked the whole hedge this morning, walked all the way around it."

"It doesn't show – you have to lean on it." I was being helpful, but you'd never know it from his face.

"Why don't we all go over there now and you can show Mr. Tomas where you mean?" Dad suggested anxiously.

I shrugged. "I don't know if I can find it again. Tell you what, it'll be near where you saw Maple's hoofprints. You'll see where she got tangled up in wire – which ought to be mended, by the way – and if you walk in a straight line through the trees from there you'll come to the broken part of the hedge."

He took a sharp breath. "I'll check it now and make immediate arrangements for its repair."

"And the broken fence wire," I said innocently. "It's really dangerous."

"Hmmm," Brad Tomas shot me a suspicious look. "It was probably broken by the previous trespasser."

"Not guilty," I smiled at him brightly. "Last night was the first time for Maple and me. I promise."

Dad saw him out to his car and came back to the study, collapsing on his chair with a groan. "What a nightmare! I know I shouldn't get so upset, Gemma, but I've told you all before, my childhood was nearly ruined by fights between my parents and the people who lived next door and it's left me with a real horror of being involved in conflict. One of the main reasons your mother and I settled here was that there has never been anything of that kind, but now – now I've got *two* neighbors gunning for me."

"They'll soon forget it," I assured him cheerfully. "It's a huge fuss about nothing; a few broken plants in one garden and hoofprints in another. Hoofprints! Duh!"

I was glad to see him give a weak smile and kept up the chatter, hoping he wouldn't ask the question that was burning holes in my own brain. Just how had Jason known about the gap in Brad Tomas's hedge? The way he'd taken me straight to it told me that he'd known its exact location and there could only be one explanation for that – he'd used it before. For some reason Jason had been inside those grounds before last night and seeing how very, very mad it had made Brad Tomas, I thought that I needed to ask Jason just exactly *why*.

CHAPTER FOUR

Craig, when he came to join us, wanted to know the same thing of course.

"So what did Brad Tomas say about Jason?" He looked hollow eyed from studying so late. "Did you give him your boyfriend's phone number so he could find out what he's up to?"

"I don't have his phone number," I said tersely.

"We – uh – didn't actually mention Jason," Dad said looking slightly defensive. "The complaint was about Maple, and she's *our* responsibility."

"Well I know that, but there's the pertinent fact that it was Jason who showed Gemma how to break into Mr. Tomas's grounds."

"We didn't break in," I objected. "The hedge was already loose."

"Yeah, and who loosened it?" Craig threw up his hands. "Look, I know you're grateful Jason helped rescue Maple, but don't you think our neighbor should know about his involvement?"

"I'm completely convinced of Jason's innocence and I'm extremely grateful to him," Dad had made his mind up.

"I can see that, and I think you've shown enough gratitude by dishing out free riding lessons – you don't need to shield him from Brad Tomas as well!"

"Mr. Tomas can make his own inquiries," Dad obviously liked the man no better than I did. "Gemma and I have apologized for entering his grounds uninvited and I shall offer to pay for the hedge repair but that's as far as we need to go, I feel."

"We think he's a bully and he's overreacting," I joined in. "It's only a little broken shrubbery and some hoofprints – big deal!"

"Suit yourselves," Craig picked up his textbooks. "But I've still got my doubts as far as Jason goes. Kids like him don't spend Saturday nights hanging around a deserted country lane for no reason."

"Your brother has a very suspicious nature," Dad watched him leave. "I'm glad to see you're more like me, Gemma."

I smiled at him and kept quiet, not letting him know I had a few concerns too.

I kept thinking about it and after Jason's second riding lesson the following day I decided that despite what Dad said I did actually want to know. The lesson had gone really well and after grooming Pearl and tidying the ring and yard, Jason was now helping me clean the paddock.

"This is the less glamorous side of owning horses," I handed him a shovel. "Though I'd rather spend time doing this than calming down the neighbors like my poor dad yesterday."

"Oh," he smiled as Logan, followed by Khan, came over to say hello. "Was Bryan Edwards still complaining?"

"He never stops, but this was someone else," I said

casually, patting Logan as I spoke. "Brad Tomas is his name."

Jason, scratching Khan between his ears, showed no reaction. "Who's he?"

"A new guy in the lane. He owns the house at the end. The one where Maple ended up."

"Ah," he dropped his head and got busy with the shovel. "I guess you told him about me then."

"No, my dad and I thought it was none of his business."

"Your dad's amazing," he looked up and his eyes were clear and candid. "I've never met anyone like him – most people take one look at me and think I'm trouble."

"And are you?" I met his gaze. "Brad Tomas says someone's been in his grounds before."

"Yeah, that was us," he took my breath away by saying. "We were only fooling around though. Vinny was trying to steal a can from me and we had a mock fight that ended with falling into that hedge and breaking the part I showed you. Vin thought it'd be a joke to go in and take a look around but we didn't damage anything."

"How did this Brad know you'd been in there then?" I was pretty sure he was telling the truth but I wanted the whole story. "He was really mad about it."

"I grabbed Vin's woolly hat and shoved it on the head of a statue – stupid looking thing. It was a little too near the house though and I triggered the security lights, so then we hoofed it."

"That all sounds pretty harmless. I don't know what the man's problem is." I hesitated. "So, just what is it that brings your – um – gang down this way? It must be a pretty boring way to spend an evening, I'd have thought."

"And you'd be right," he moved the wheelbarrow very quietly so as not to alarm Khan. "I think this horse is great, you know. I mean, I think they're all great but there's something about Khan."

"He's certainly taken to you," I smiled at the way Khan was nuzzling his arm. "Maybe it won't be long before you can ride him."

"Yeah?" His face lit up with an almost luminous glow. "I would *love* that. I worry that it's too much work for Pearl, getting burdened with me and my lessons at her age."

"She seems to be enjoying it. I'll let you know when she's had enough." I realized he'd made another neat body swerve around the question. "Of course Craig would have to give his approval if I thought you were ready to ride his horse."

"Mm, he's not very likely to do that. Your brother doesn't like me much, does he?"

"Well," I tried again, "I think he'd be happier about having you around if he knew more about you."

"What – my life story?" Jason was being deliberately flippant. "It's the usual stuff, started as a baby, grew some – you know, that kind of thing."

"Very informative," I picked a handful of grass and threw it at him.

"Be careful!" He made a big fuss over Khan. "You're frightening my friend here."

"Will you stop clowning around," I said, starting to lose patience. "Just tell me what you were doing here on Saturday night so I can put Craig's mind at rest."

"Honestly, Gemma, he's got nothing to worry about. I

agree with your dad, the gate must have swung open by accident. Vinny, the other guys and I were just hanging around waiting for his brother."

"Vinny's brother?" I stared at him.

"Yeah, his name's Danny and it wasn't him who let the horses out either, if that's what you're thinking. Danny's older – about eighteen – and he sometimes gives us a lift in his car. Last week he had some business to sort out with a guy who works in the gas station on Brigham Road. He didn't want us hanging around so he dropped us off at the top of the lane and then came back for us."

"Was that the night you got into Brad Tomas's place?"

"Yeah, but it was only the garden, remember – we weren't breaking into the house or anything. On Saturday Danny was taking us to the other side of Brigham when this guy phoned him and said they needed to meet, so Dan did the same again and left us at the junction while he went on. There was some problem, don't know what it was, and he was much longer this time."

"So what did you all do?" I was watching him closely.

"Nothing. We just hung out getting bored till you turned up."

I recalled how quick he'd been to help Maple and gave him my best and, hopefully, most bewitching smile.

"That's better," he grinned back. "First time I saw you I knew you'd be a knock-out when you smiled."

I blushed, feeling suddenly, incredibly happy. To hide the fact I pelted him with grass again and he retaliated this time. We kept on goofing around while we cleared the rest of the field until, to my surprise, Craig yelled from the fence, "Gem, are you and Logan coming out with me or not?"

"I didn't realize it was so late. We were supposed to be riding to the common," I told Jason. We started hurrying back while Jason trundled the full wheelbarrow. "Do you want me to mention about you riding Khan?"

"Nah," he gave a somber, hooded glance across the paddock. "Wait till Craig's made his mind up whether he trusts me enough. You're all right with me though, aren't you?"

"Absolutely," I said fervently. "And I like giving you lessons and I *really* like getting some help around the place."

"Great," the smile returned. "I'll empty this wheelbarrow out and get going but I'll see you tomorrow, OK?"

"OK." I practically soared over the grass, light footed with happiness, and hopped over the fence into the yard.

"Come on Craig," I gave his arm a flick. "Let's get these horses tacked up."

Khan was very excited when we set out for the common, prancing and pulling.

"He doesn't go out enough," I looked at my brother critically. "Don't hold him so tight. You're making him worse."

"Hey," he was annoyed. "You're not *my* teacher, you know! Just because you can boss Lover Boy around –"

"Stop making cracks like that! It's not funny," I snapped back. "Jason's not my boyfriend but I'm still glad it's him I'm teaching and not *you*. At least he's willing to put in some work!"

We bickered all the way to the common, something we do pretty often. Dad says we started fighting as soon as I learned to talk and that we haven't stopped since, but as soon as we hit open country we shut up and got on with enjoying ourselves. The rough landscape was bathed in early evening light, the sun on its slow descent throwing long shadows of inky purple. Khan, desperate to gallop, took some holding as we trotted, and then cantered to warm up. As soon as his hooves touched the broad swathe of turf he recognized as a galloping trail, he was off. I moved Logan alongside, matching the black horse's stride, but didn't try to make a race of it, knowing the youngster was already way too excited. Despite the upward incline sloping away from us Khan showed no sign of wanting to stop but finally listened to Craig's aids and began the downward transition into canter. I thought my brother was doing fine and slowed Logan too, enjoying the smooth, effortless way he tempered his speed, flowing seamlessly through the paces. Just ahead of us, Khan seemed to be doing OK too till a sudden movement, maybe a bird or a rabbit in the undergrowth, made him swerve suddenly. Craig lost his stirrups and very nearly his seat, tipping out of the saddle and almost over his horse's head. Khan, whether frightened or just being naughty, responded by bucking violently, giving my poor brother absolutely no chance of staying put. He shot through the air and Khan bucked again before taking off, reins and stirrup leathers flapping wildly.

It seems unkind to say my first thought was for the horse, rather than Craig, but it's true. There was no knowing what sort of trouble the inexperienced and highly strung Khan might get into, so I put Logan into a gallop and chased after the black horse immediately.

The ground beneath us was still soft, yielding turf but the trail had narrowed dramatically so at first all I could do was stay close to Khan's flowing tail and wait for an opportunity to move alongside. He didn't handle the winding, twisting trail as well as my boy, stumbling several times and veering off course onto rough vegetation. I spoke his name, my voice calm and soothing, in the hopes he'd listen and stop this mindless, headlong running. Logan was wonderful, keeping his pace steady until it was safe to pull out and move up. He has the amazing ability to keep a little speed in reserve, and he now put it into use, gliding swiftly forward until his head was in line with Khan's. I saw the naughty boy roll an eye and try to surge away, but with the lightest of touches Logan increased his speed too. He did it so smoothly I could lean across and reach Khan's reins while still talking to him.

"Whoa, Khan, steady boy. Whoa now."

Gradually the runaway dropped his pace; cantering in time with Logan who maintained his silky rhythm and harmony until at last we stopped. Khan's sides were heaving and his neck was soaked with sweat but he seemed unharmed as he leaned his nose against his friend.

"You're a silly boy," I told him sternly, leaning over to pat him gently. "What was all that about?"

I walked them both back, leading the now quiet and acquiescent black pony, and was glad to see Craig making his way toward us. His shirt and jodhpurs were dirty and he had a long scratch on one arm but the main injury was to his pride.

"I can't believe he got rid of me," he said and bent to check his horse's legs. "I never fall off."

"Not since before Christmas," I agreed innocently and laughed when he glared up at me. "Oh come on, Craig, Khan can be a handful. It wasn't your fault."

He climbed stiffly back into the saddle and said ruefully, "Maybe you were right about putting more work in."

"Mm," my brain was ticking away. "Still, once Jason's mastered the basics maybe he can help. He and Khan get along really well and –"

"And he's a total beginner and I don't *want* him riding my horse," Craig's glare was angrier than before. "Just because you and Dad think the guy's some kind of hero doesn't mean we all have to give him everything he wants."

"Oh here we go," I said, instantly on the defensive. "You're being irrational just because you don't like Jason."

"I don't *know* Jason and neither do you." He winced as he rubbed his arm.

"Well, I'm *getting* to know him. He's a genuine guy, Craig. He really loves horses and wants to learn all about them."

"He's not a little kid. How come he hasn't learned about them before? And anyway, we still don't know what he was doing hanging around here on Saturday."

"Yes we do," I quickly filled him in with the details about Vinny's brother.

"I'm not convinced," he said, so stubborn I could scream, "but if you want to waste your time teaching him to ride it's up to you. There's no way I'm going to let him try Khan – for a start the horse is way too difficult for a novice."

Inwardly I cursed for getting my timing so wrong but I consoled myself that Jason's lessons would still go ahead. If it became too much work for Pearl I'd even put him up on my beloved Logan, with me in control on the lunge rein if necessary. Jason certainly seemed totally committed, arriving every day that week for his lesson in the ring and putting in a lot of hard work with any chores that needed doing. Craig, very pointedly, kept out of his way and Mom, too, was less welcoming than I'd hoped.

"I think you should tell Jason to stay away this weekend," she said on Friday. "Tessa and Sonny are coming over and I'd prefer it to be just family."

"But those two don't have anything to do with the horses," I objected. "Tessa goes out to say hello to them but Sonny doesn't even do that. They'll hardly know Jason's here."

"It's actually because of the horses that they're coming," she surprised me by saying. "Tessa was really upset about them getting out and Maple going missing. I'm not so sure Sonny wants to come. He gets bored, I think."

"He shouldn't bother then," I said ungraciously. "I'd much rather have Jason here than Sonny."

"There's room for everyone," Dad, the peacemaker, said, generous as usual. "I'll ask Sonny to fix my computer. He likes that."

"And I want to give Jason a lungeing lesson on Logan so Pearl can have a day off."

"Oh, all right," Mom good naturedly gave in. "But let's make sure this is a nice peaceful weekend after the last horror – we don't want any more upsets like that again."

In the beginning, it seemed Mom was going to get her wish. Tessa, who was much more concerned about the horses than I'd imagined, spent a lot of time with them while Dad distracted her boyfriend with the computer. My sister met Jason who, having put in a very well balanced performance in the lunge lesson, had cleaned the field and then spent ages doing some repair work on the shelter.

"He's *really* nice," she gave me a quick hug as we helped Mom with supper. "Kind of reserved, but there are hidden depths I think, Gemma."

"Oh, not you too!" Craig came into the room and scowled at both of us. "Don't tell me you've signed up as a member of the Jason Fan Club."

"How come you've got a problem with him?" She looked surprised. "Are you getting grouchy in your old age, Craig?"

"You're the oldest remember, Tessa," he gave the automatic response to her teasing. "There's nothing wrong with me. I just don't want to give a whole-hearted welcome to a complete stranger, that's all."

"He won't *be* a stranger if you get to know him," Tessa pointed out acerbically. "I think all that studying must be addling your brain!"

"Just what I said," I grinned at her. "He hasn't got time for anything except his books and Buster. He doesn't even bother with his horse half the time."

"Listen to you!" Craig glared at me again. "Next you'll be getting Tessa to bully me into letting your precious Jason ride Khan."

"My fiancée doesn't *do* bullying," Sonny strolled in.

"Anyway, the way your dad's been singing the guy's praises I'd have thought you'd be glad to have him exercise your horse."

Craig controlled his temper with an obvious effort. "For one – Jason is a complete novice and two – I'm not convinced I want him around."

"Oh?" Sonny seemed interested. "Is this because of the neighbor trouble? I've never seen your dad so upset. He says one of the reasons you've all stayed here so long is the good relationship you've had with the other residents on the lane."

"I wouldn't call it a relationship exactly." I just couldn't help arguing with Sonny. "We hardly ever *see* any of them."

"And that's exactly how I like it," Dad joined us. "A friendly hello when we meet, but mostly we don't bother them and they don't bother us."

"Except when there's something to complain about," Sonny said as he stepped around Scala, carefully avoiding touching her. "They certainly reacted harshly over your horses' bid for freedom."

I didn't bother telling him our four weren't trying to escape or anything; they simply wandered out of an open gate.

"It's all OK again," I said, not wanting Dad to dwell on the subject. "Bryan Edwards' garden is replanted and Brad Tomas had his hedge repaired so they'll both forget it now."

"I hope so." Sonny removed a cat from his chair. "I'd hate you to be hounded out by angry neighbors."

"Maybe it wouldn't be a bad thing," Craig couldn't

agree with *anyone,* it seemed. "If Mom and Dad sell this place and buy something smaller, there'd be enough money for me to start my own veterinary practice when I qualify."

"Yeah, like that's going to happen!" I gave Buster a tidbit and told the little dog, "Your owner's missing some marbles, isn't he?"

As we all dug into Mom's delicious food the bickering soon stopped and we enjoyed the usual happy, noisy mealtime our family loves. Craig, with a heroic effort, even delayed his evening study session to join in a few silly games before disappearing with his books and his dog. I had an hour or so on the computer, searching for training tips for Jason's next riding lesson. Yawning, I switched it off and went to get boots and a flashlight for the late night horse check. It was now exactly a week since those dreadful few minutes I'd spent crashing around their deserted field and I felt a cold trickle of fear at the too-fresh memory. Just as I opened the back door I heard the sound of running footsteps pounding along our driveway and my stomach lurched convulsively as the panic-fueled thought hit me – "Not again! Oh please, *please* not again!"

CHAPTER FIVE

"Ken! Ken!" It was Sonny, yelling for my dad.

As he ran nearer, the house lights picked up his expression, tense and alarmed.

"Are the horses all right?" I practically screamed and he blinked bewilderedly.

"I guess so."

"What's happened?" Dad, his hair sticking up in a fluffy halo, came out of the front door.

"I heard something," Sonny turned toward him. "Craig did too – he's checking the lane."

"The horses!" It was my only thought and I ran madly to the field gate.

It was shut and firmly locked and to my utter relief my flashlight beam showed the four horses safely grazing inside the paddock. I leaned against a fence post until the panicky hammering of my heart quieted. Dad, still wearing his slippers, padded up to join me, his worried frown lifting when he saw my face.

"They're OK? Thank –"

"Dad?" Craig appeared out of the dark. "Have you seen anyone? I ran along the lane but there's no one around. He could have doubled back –"

"He? Who?" I asked stupidly and Craig hesitated.

"Whoever dug up the plants – look," he switched his flashlight back on and shone it downwards.

A trail of scattered earth littered the road and just inside the entrance to our drive a couple of uprooted shrubs lay in a tangled heap.

Dad swept a hand through his already crazy hair. "How did they get there?"

"Someone yanked them up from Bryan Edwards' garden and dumped them on us," Craig focused his flashlight light to show us the vandal's route, marked by clods of fallen earth and scattered leaves from the plants.

I felt as puzzled as Dad looked and felt complete sympathy for him when he let out a low groan, "But *why*?"

"More trouble making," Craig said bitterly. "Someone thinks it's funny to stir things up again by making it look as though *we're* wrecking Bryan's garden."

"That's ridiculous," Dad bent to examine the shrubs. "You're right though, these have only recently been planted, I bought them to replace the ones the horses damaged. They've still got labels on them, look."

"That's really spiteful," I shook my head. "I mean, it's hardly in the same category as letting the horses out but it's still nasty. Is it someone with a grudge against Bryan Edwards?"

"I think it's directed more at us," Craig sounded grim. "Otherwise why dump the evidence on our property?"

Poor Dad looked totally shocked. "Why? *Why* would they do that?"

"Don't upset yourself, Ken," Sonny patted his arm. "I'm sure no one's trying to pick a fight with you."

We spent what seemed like half the night debating the issue, with everyone but my belligerent brother, trying to defuse Dad's agitation. Craig's only concession was to suggest sneaking into our neighbor's garden, replanting the shrubs and cleaning up the mess so he wouldn't know about it, but Dad said the plan was underhanded.

"Honesty is always the best policy," he said firmly. "I'll pay Bryan a visit first thing in the morning, tell him what happened and that we're completely mystified by it."

"All right," Mom planted a kiss on his forehead. "But you need to stop worrying. I can't believe there's anyone with a vendetta against us. It's probably just somebody with a warped sense of humor playing what they think is a joke."

"Yeah?" Craig looked really tired. "In which case Gemma had better find out from her boyfriend what he and his little gang were up to tonight."

"Oh don't start!" I'd been wondering how long it would be before he began blaming Jason. "He doesn't *do* stuff like this. Just give him a break, will you!"

I wasn't sure how I was going to approach the subject with Jason without making it sound like an accusation but he arrived so early he met Dad in the lane on his way back from Bryan Edwards's.

"That was kinda weird last night," he said, picking up a grooming kit. "I bet your brother thought it was me trouble making, didn't he?"

"Uh," I was taken aback by his directness. "No. Well – he sort of wondered –"

"Not guilty," he held his free hand up. "Danny drove us over to see the new movie way over on the other side of town. They were showing a cult martial arts film that he and Vinny were dying to see. I thought it was stupid, but I didn't sneak out to run ten miles across Brigham to do some midnight gardening across the road."

58

"It wasn't midnight, only about ten thirty," I said absently. "Sonny and Craig heard someone but they didn't catch him. It seems such a pointless thing for anyone to do."

"It riled up that guy Edwards again though, didn't it? Your dad said he was hopping mad and was taking it out on your family. Maybe someone around here is trying to do just that – cause a neighborhood war. In which case my money would be on Brad Tomas."

"Brad – why on earth –?"

"Oh I don't know *why*," he slid an arm lovingly around Khan's neck. "Maybe he's just a psycho. I mean, look at the way he overreacted about Maple. And about us having a joke with his statue."

"Yes he did seem more angry than reasonable," I said slowly. "Even my dad thought so. He said Brad was the most unreasonable man he'd ever met."

"There you go, then – he's a nut case, and only a nut case would pull a stunt like last night."

"Craig said it must have been the same person who let the horses out last week," I watched him gently but efficiently brush the dirt from Khan's coat.

"So in other words he's still got me down as number one suspect." He didn't stop brushing.

"No," I said slowly. "My brother's stubborn but he's not stupid. He can see you wouldn't do anything to harm the horses."

"I wouldn't do anything to cause trouble here, period," he said and looked up at me. "I'd be crazy to, wouldn't I? I still can't believe you're letting me do all this, so there's no way I'd mess it up with a stupid game like last night.

Your dad's really upset. He hates the idea that someone's got it in for him and I'd never do anything to make him feel like that after he's treated me so well."

It was the most personal speech I'd heard him make and he spoke with genuine passion.

"Let's forget it," I said, determined to lighten the atmosphere. "I've got something a little different planned for today."

"Yeah?" His gorgeous dark eyes were bright.

"Pearl's absolutely fine, and after a day without any work she could do with some exercise and a little variety. So instead of a ring session, how about a ride on the common?"

"Fantastic!" His good-looking face shone with enthusiasm.

Craig, as usual, found fault with my plan.

"I wanted to ride this morning," he said, still hollow eyed. "But no doubt Jason's more important than Khan and me."

"There's nothing to stop you coming along with us," I smiled sweetly at him. "It'll be a quiet ride of course, but you and your horse could do with going back to basics."

"Thanks, but no thanks," he whistled to Buster and went back to the house without, I noticed crossly, stopping to see Khan.

Pearl was delighted to be going out, arching her silver neck and blowing excitedly down her nose as we left the yard.

"She's gorgeous," Jason patted her affectionately. "I just hope I don't spoil her day!"

"You won't." I was totally confident. "You've got

60

terrific natural balance and you know how to use your hands so you won't be jabbing her in the mouth or bouncing around and making her back sore."

He really did look great, sitting lightly in the saddle, his back straight, yet supple so his hips and waist could follow the rhythm of Pearl's natural movement. Logan led the way, with the gray mare keeping in line behind us. The gate at the edge of the common is slightly tricky for Pearl because of her long back but I explained how to approach it and was pleased by the way Jason sat quietly and let the horse take her time.

"It's designed to keep cars and motorcycles from coming in here." I swept an arm to point out the view. "It works really well. You'll only see walkers and horses enjoying the place."

"It's great." His face, often moody and shuttered, was a picture of animation. "I haven't been here in years. I'd forgotten how big and wild it is."

"Don't you spend much time outdoors?" I still knew next to nothing about his life.

The heavy lids dropped to veil his eyes. "Not a lot. The park in Brigham, that's about it, I guess."

"Oh." We live only a few miles from the town, so I know it's not deep in the heart of the countryside or anything, but I love the fact that we've got this rough, natural expanse of land within easy reach. "My family and I come out here quite a lot."

"Yeah, your dad told me your dogs get a walk on the common most days."

"We bring them out with the horses sometimes too, but Scala's getting a little old for that now and Buster's a

61

lunatic – he keeps disappearing after rabbits, so I decided against it today."

"It's terrific like this, just you, me and the horses," he flashed the grin that made my legs wobble. "Can we trot or –"

"A little more walking to warm them up properly," I tried to concentrate on being a teacher, "then I want to see you give the correct aids."

Pearl was contentedly following Logan and I wanted to see how much control Jason had without getting a lead from my pony. The gray mare was slightly reluctant to move ahead, hanging back when he first asked her to go on, but he tried again and made a creditable transition to rising trot. Today wasn't the most exciting riding I'd ever enjoyed. Logan and I tend to go for the cross country approach; a trail ride across the common, cantering, galloping and jumping, but I thoroughly enjoyed the far more sedate hour we spent with Jason. I didn't tell him that I'd coiled a lead rope into my pocket in case he had trouble motivating Pearl because it never became necessary to use it.

"A week ago I'd never have believed this," he remarked, then asked Pearl to wait while Logan and I negotiated the gate. "Me riding a horse – *me*!"

"You're a natural." I wasn't being flattering, just telling the absolute truth. "Not everyone takes to it the way you have."

I was pleased at the way he looked after Pearl when he took her back to her stable and would have liked to spend more time with him, just chilling out with the horses, but I was under strict orders from Mom not to be late for lunch.

"Tessa and Sonny are leaving this afternoon so I want us all to be together before they go," she'd told me.

I personally thought Sonny wouldn't even notice if I wasn't at the table but Tessa had been terrific this visit, much more like the sister I remembered before she took off for the city, so I'd agreed. Jason tactfully said he had to go too.

"Are you stuck like me?" I covered my curiosity with a bright smile. "Stuck with going to a boring family lunch?"

"I don't think so. It depends on how well my sister is."

"Oh, I didn't know she was sick –" I began when Craig stuck his head out of the back door and yelled, "Gemma! Come on!"

"Enjoy your meal," Jason vaulted over the carefully locked paddock gate and picked up his bike. "Can I come over after school tomorrow?"

"Absolutely." I vowed silently to continue the conversation about his sister. "At this rate you'll soon be *galloping* across that common!"

He grinned and took off, and I stood and watched him, pretty soppily I must admit. Lunch was OK, with nice food as usual, but the conversation was pretty dull and I stopped listening and drifted off into my own, much better, thoughts. Sonny and Craig were talking business, dull stuff about possible premises for an animal hospital, plus the usual house versus apartment thing Sonny's always yammering on about.

"Whatever you do, don't rent, always buy," Sonny was saying. "You have to get your feet on the property ladder."

"But you need a lot of money for a deposit, don't you?" Mom was in her element with all the family around her and didn't seem to mind how boring the subject was.

I yawned and entered my favorite daydream where Jason and I rode side by side across fields, streams and woodland.

"She's in a little world of her own," Tessa leaned across and shook me playfully. "Wake up, Gemma! We're discussing the wedding and you should have some say since you're going to be bridesmaid."

"Hm," I wasn't too sure about that. "As long as you don't dress me in something pink and frilly."

"You'd look gorgeous," Mom said immediately and Dad beamed at me proudly.

"Gem's concerned about what *Jason* would say," Craig couldn't resist a jibe. "He's a cool street dude or whatever they call it in the city – I can't see him liking Gem in a frilly frock."

"Don't listen to him, it won't be like that," Tessa bashed our brother none too gently.

"It won't be like *anything* until we've got a lot more cash," said Sonny. He never joined in our clowning. "I want it all to be perfect and that costs."

I personally thought that if you really wanted to marry someone you should just do it regardless of perfection but it wasn't my place to say so. Tessa came out with me to the paddock later and spent ages saying goodbye to the horses but I could see Sonny was itching to get away. He practically dragged Tessa to the car and I could see the relief on his face when they drove away, Tessa beside him madly waving and blowing kisses.

"I'm going to take Khan out," my brother surprised me by saying. "I don't want him developing bad habits like he showed yesterday."

"I'll come with you if you like," I offered. "Logan only walked and trotted this morning. He'd enjoy a bigger challenge."

"Great," Craig obviously didn't bear a grudge that I'd preferred Jason's company earlier. "Let's go now, OK?"

"Are you taking the dogs?" Dad enquired, patting the ever-present Scala.

"No, I want to concentrate on Khan if that's all right. Buster's asleep in his bed in my room – I'll take him out later," said Craig.

We brought the two horses into the yard, got them ready, and were cantering across the common twenty minutes later. Khan pulled like a train again but I bit my tongue and didn't criticize, seeing how hard Craig was trying. I thought he was too heavy handed. Khan's mouth is very sensitive and he frequently threw his head up in an effort to avoid the strong pressure on the bit. The black horse was better behaved though, especially after we'd enjoyed a good gallop, and as soon as my brother relaxed and softened Khan stopped jogging and tugging.

"We're not as good a partnership as you and Logan though, are we?" Craig said ruefully as we turned for home. "It's amazing how well you're attuned to each other."

"Thanks," I said and hugged my pony's neck. "Some of that is just natural but a lot of hard work goes into it too."

"Yeah I know, and you're right, I should put in the

hours with Khan. I'm finding the studying hard, Gem, and I'm scared that even if I qualify no one will want to take me on as a vet."

"Of course they will." I stared at him. "Is that why you were joining in with all that yak about property with Sonny?"

"If I could afford to buy my own practice I wouldn't have to worry," he said simply. "But I can't see Dad selling the house to finance me."

"Why should he?" I thought he was way out of line. "We love living here, and where would the animals go if Mom and Dad spent the money on your business and Tessa's wedding? It's not as if we could fit in a little apartment somewhere."

He looked gloomier than ever and I wished he'd be more positive about his exams and his future in general. It had been a nice ride though and despite my brother driving me nuts sometimes I'm pretty fond of him so I didn't nag, and instead cheered him up by letting him and Khan beat us in a race back along the galloping trail. By the time we'd walked our horses over the last stretch of common and back along the lane Craig was super cheerful, laughing his head off at my attempts to sing and looking more relaxed than he had in ages. The evening sun was low in the sky as we turned into our driveway – and I felt my heart lurch downwards to join it. Pulled up outside the front door was the sleek, expensive car belonging to Brad Tomas.

"Uh-oh," Craig's face fell too. "What's he come to moan about now? Put Khan away for me so I can sneak back to my room without seeing him, OK Gem?"

"No," I couldn't believe his nerve. "You rode him so making him comfortable is your job. Brad Tomas won't want to see you anyway. He's probably found another hoofprint from last week."

I actually thought that the man must have discovered Jason was now a frequent visitor here and wanted to interrogate him about the "hat and statue" incident.

"Craig!" Dad sounded really agitated. "In here, please!"

Craig looked across to where Dad stood at the front door. "Let me put Khan in his stable and I'll be right there."

"Why does he want you?" I was agog. "What have you done?"

Craig shook his head and went to un-tack his horse. He covered the black pony with an anti-sweat rug so I swiftly did the same for Logan and hurried out of his stable.

"You don't need to come," my brother said but I grinned at him.

"I'm giving you moral support."

"Yeah and being nosy at the same time," he grinned back. "Come on then, let's see what complaint our new neighbor has dreamed up now."

We both thought it would be some trivial little problem and were totally unprepared to be greeted by a sour faced Brad Tomas who stood up and snarled, "Well? I hope you've got a good explanation for this because I'm telling you now, if I find your dog on my grounds again I'll shoot him!"

CHAPTER SIX

Buster, as if he understood every word, wriggled out of Mom's arms and flung himself at Craig.

"What did you say?" My brother cradled the squirming terrier close against him.

"Mr. Tomas found Buster inside his grounds," Mom said quickly. "And he's most concerned –"

"I'm more than concerned, I am furious. There's no way that animal could have wandered in by accident. We made sure the hedge and fence are impenetrable."

"So how do you think he did it?" Craig's eyes were glittering. "Through the gate?"

"The gate is electronically locked and completely solid. I suggest the only way that dog got through was by being carried, deliberately carried by someone, which means that yet again your family has been trespassing on my property."

"That's a load of garbage," Craig said bluntly. "I suppose you mean me, but for a start I've been out riding on the common and even if I hadn't I wouldn't be wasting precious study time sneaking my dog into your garden. What would be the point?"

Brad Tomas hesitated, licking his lips. "You tell me."

"Look," I said, trying to act peacemaker like Dad usually does. "We went out on our horses and left Buster here. He probably woke up and realized Craig had gone so somehow he got out and tried to find him, that's all. He's so small he could easily squeeze through your hedge –"

"No he couldn't," Brad said sharply. "And anyway, to echo your brother's sentiment – why would he? You were riding on the common so why would your dog go chasing off in pursuit, yet take completely the wrong direction?"

"Buster's not too smart," Craig smiled down at the dog who licked him ecstatically. "And I'm really sorry he went the wrong way and got into your garden but I promise you it wasn't deliberate. Did he cause any damage?"

"Not that I saw," Brad said stiffly. "Though a certain amount of trampling took place while we tried to catch him."

I quickly hid a smile with my hand, picturing the little terrier evading everyone who was running after him.

"Sorry," Craig said again. "It was a complete accident and it won't happen again."

"I believe that's what you assured me last week," the man snatched up his car keys. "It strikes me as extremely suspicious that all your animals make a beeline for my place whenever you're careless enough to let them run amok."

Dad, his face unusually grim, said nothing and it was left to Mom to apologize again and to see Brad out with assurances that we'd be much more careful in the future.

"Well!" She came back into the room and glared at Dad. "You weren't much help, Ken!"

"I said sorry," he said defensively. "And Craig said sorry – what else does the man want? Threatening to shoot our dog – how could he!"

"He's making out like we've got some sort of

campaign to get inside his property – what the heck is all that about?" Craig put Buster on the floor. "What's so special about it that he doesn't want even a small terrier wandering through the fence?"

"We *were* in the wrong though," Mom pointed out. "So for goodness' sake make sure nothing else happens to upset either Brad or Bryan. We've never had trouble with neighbors before and I don't want any more!"

Dad, obviously badly shaken, said, "It's my childhood all over again. I can't bear it, and if it gets any worse I'd have to leave, I really would."

He took Scala off for one of their long walks to try and calm himself down while Craig, accompanied by Buster of course, went back to the yard. Feeling seriously perturbed I went with them to sort out our horses.

"Brad Tomas really upset my Dad over it, but I think the whole thing was kind of weird," I finished telling Jason the story the next day. "I mean, Buster's never gone missing from the house before. We lose him on the common sometimes but he always tracks Craig down in the end."

"He was definitely inside Brad Tomas's place?" Jason leaned thoughtfully on his shovel.

"I guess. The guy brought him back here because he read our address on his collar."

"Brad could have just found him in the lane and cooked up the story to start another fight."

"That doesn't make sense," I objected. "Your theory was he wanted to cause trouble between Bryan Edwards and us, so how does this fit in?"

"Maybe Brad wants you out," he smiled as the black

horse came over to greet him. "Hello Khan, how are you? And before you ask *why*, Gemma, I don't know. It's just a theory, like before."

"I prefer your other idea – that Brad's some kind of psycho," I gave Logan a mint I'd found in my pocket, "Because it's all crazy, no matter how you look at it."

"There's another angle, of course. You said your brother liked the idea of your parents selling and contributing to his practice – maybe *he's* the one digging up plants and shoving his dog inside gardens."

"Craig?" I glared at him. "Now you really are talking trash."

He shrugged. "You said you wanted input, I'm only trying to help."

"Well you're not," I pushed away the nagging doubt about Craig that was beginning to build in my mind. "Let's forget it; it's just another hassle over nothing. How was your sister yesterday?"

"OK," he stopped to make a fuss over Maple, "It was one of her better days so I helped Mom take her to the park."

"Is she little?"

"No, she's only a couple of years younger than I am but she's disabled so we have to use a wheelchair."

"Oh, I'm sorry." I felt guilty, babbling on about trivial fights with neighbors when his family had *real* problems. "Was she in an accident or something?"

"No, it's a medical condition she was born with. Mom's always been her full time caregiver – it's hard."

"It must be difficult for you," I said, thinking of my own full, happy life. "If you want to bring your Mom and sister over to meet the horses –"

His voice was polite but his expression remained shuttered. "That's kind of you, but Helen's allergic. I even have to change my clothes in the shed when I leave here so I don't bring horse or dog hair into the house."

"Oh I see. I wondered why you'd never had anything to do with horses before when you like them so much."

"Now you know." He picked up the wheelbarrow and started moving it briskly away.

I knew it was his way of ending the conversation, and changed the subject right away.

"Would you give me a hand with some loose schooling in a minute, Jason?"

As always, when it came to anything involving the horses, he became a different person. He immediately dropped the aloof, defensive attitude and started asking questions, his good-looking face alive with interest.

"Bring Khan in," I slipped a head collar on Logan. "And I'll show you what it's all about."

Before I learned to lunge my pony I'd put in a lot of work loose schooling him. It's a good, gentle way of teaching a horse to respond to voice commands and I think it develops a real empathy between the two of you. By now my beautiful iron gray boy would perform almost any discipline I asked, and Jason watched spellbound as Logan trotted and cantered around the ring. I got him jumping too, over an inviting oval shaped lane of small, solid fences, so that I could evaluate his action. Having sent him around in one direction two or three times, I stopped and rewarded him, then asked him to do the course the other way around.

"This improves Logan's balance and means he's comfortable on either bend," I told Jason.

"He obviously loves it too," he said, unable tear his eyes away. "I had no idea horses could do this. I read the books you lent me all the time but I haven't seen any mention of it."

"The ones I let you borrow are text books, designed to instruct the rider, whereas what we're doing today comes under the heading of training the horse, I guess." I brought my clever pony quietly to a halt and made a big fuss over him. "I'll leave the jumps up so I can ride him around later but I'd like to try Khan now that you're here to help."

"You're going to get him jumping too?" He was excited.

"'Fraid not," I smiled ruefully. "Khan hasn't actually gotten the hang of loose schooling and usually ignores me completely. Craig's never bothered with it but I'm a firm believer and think it will help."

"Tell me what to do."

"Lead him quietly in the ring and walk him onto the track." I indicated the trodden path around the outer edge. "In theory all I have to do once you've detached the lead rope is walk the diagonals, keeping slightly behind Khan's eye."

Jason led the black horse forward and I said firmly, "Walk on," just as he clipped the rope free. Because Khan hadn't yet learned to respond to voice only I kept it short and simple, suiting my commands to his actions initially so that he knew what each word meant. He tried to break away at one point but Jason's calm presence seemed to help and when I saw him slowing I said the word, "Halt," very clearly.

"It's not exactly rocket science," I watched with pleasure as Jason praised him. "But a few ten-minute sessions, little and often, will soon mean he'll respond perfectly to voice commands."

"You said he had a sensitive mouth," Jason led Khan away as I prepared Logan for his ridden exercises. "So teaching him this will mean Craig can use a much lighter touch when he's riding doesn't it?"

"That's the idea," I agreed, thinking privately it would be a big help if my brother joined in with the training.

Jason seemed to enjoy watching Logan and me handle the little jump course and I could tell he was making mental notes of everything we did.

"I've got a lot to learn," he said, giving us a round of applause when we finished our session. "But I'm loving every minute."

"Great," I grinned at him. "I'll clean Logan up and then we can put them both back in the field and get Pearl ready for you."

Singing softly, (well I wouldn't want to put Jason off by letting him hear me!), I brushed Logan down and left his stable to return the saddle to our tack room. The sand ring is just a short distance from the yard and to my surprise it was being used. Jason and Khan were repeating the exercises I'd done earlier, but to my amazement the black pony was now foot perfect, showing no sign of running out, standing defiantly still, or generally playing up as he always did with me. It was an extraordinarily touching sight, the tall, dark-haired Jason moving and speaking softly, in complete accord with the equally dark and stunning horse, and I felt a lump of emotion forming in my throat. Jason finished the session by calling Khan to him, achieving an immediate, perfect response that ended with Khan dropping his soft nose almost into the palm of his hand.

I waited till he'd fixed the lead rope and called, "Well done! You're showing me up now."

"Duh! Don't think so!" he was smiling all over his face. "But thanks anyway. This horse is just *amazing*."

"I don't think Craig would always agree," I pictured the disgruntled expression when he'd fallen off. "But you and Khan seem to have clicked in a big way, haven't you? Come on, let's go and get Pearl."

The riding lesson went well too and I was taken with the way Jason spent time with all the horses after the teaching sessions were over.

"I thought it was only me who liked just *being* with my horse friends," I smiled a bit self consciously as we lay on the grass only inches away from the four contented ponies.

"No, I love it too," he smiled as Maple blew curiously into his face. "And apart from worrying about keeping horse hair out of the house, my Mom's all for it too."

"Yeah?" I was curious since he so rarely volunteered information like that. "How come?"

"She says Khan, Logan, Maple and Pearl are preferable company to Vin, Danny, Rick and Mac."

"Oh right," I laughed. "I don't know them of course but I thought Vinny looked a bit – scary."

"He's all right. Both the Jameson brothers are pretty harmless, but they seem to attract trouble somehow. I've gotten used to being judged the same way, so it's nice to be treated like a regular person for a change."

"By your horse friends, you mean?" I teased him. "They think you're a lot better than that – oh and my dad and I rate you pretty highly as well."

"Thanks!" He reached out and ruffled my hair.

"Gemma!" Craig, as he often did these days, sounded irked. "You'd better come in; your supper's been ready for a while."

"I've got homework too," I told Jason. "So I'd better go."

We'd already compared notes on our schools and I was annoyed that I had a lot more subjects to wrestle with than he did.

As we reached the gate I said, "See you tomorrow?"

"You sure?" he still seemed amazed that I kept asking him back.

"Sure," I said lightly. "You're probably going to end up some kind of riding star so I want to be able to say it's all due to my brilliant teaching."

I tried not to watch him leave this time, realizing I was getting seriously hooked, but couldn't resist a last look as he rode his bike toward the Brigham road.

"Don't let Mom catch you swooning over him like that," Craig scowled as he approached.

I stuck my tongue out and refused to let him rile me.

"I don't suppose," he said casually. "That you know the names of those brothers you mentioned – the ones who give Jason a lift sometimes?"

"It's Jameson," I said. "Why?"

"I wanted to let Sonny know," he gave me a sidelong glance. "I've asked him to do some checking."

"I wouldn't have told you Jason's last name if I'd

known that," I said angrily. "I bet you've already given Sonny all his details, haven't you?"

"Why not? If he's got nothing to hide, Sonny won't find anything."

"You shouldn't do stuff like this," I said, now really mad. "Spying on people! I like Jason and I like him being here. He's great with the horses – much better than you!"

"Thanks, Gem, it's nice to hear such strong family loyalty," he said sarcastically as he whistled to Buster and stomped away, leaving me fuming.

I thought he was way out of line and decided to ignore him from now on, but as the days passed and he didn't make any comment, I confronted him.

"So, how much dirt did Sonny dig up then? You haven't thrown Jason off our land for his criminal past, I notice."

"His friends' names showed up, but no, your boyfriend seems to be in the clear," Craig was looking more exhausted than ever. "But I'm still not changing my mind about letting him ride Khan. Once my exams are over I'll have plenty of free time so I can put more school work in."

"We've already done tons for you," I was annoyed that he was being so stubborn. "Khan will do anything for Jason."

He made an even grouchier face and went back to his seemingly endless studying. As the weekend approached I found I was getting pretty tense myself. Jason and I planned to spend most of Saturday giving all four horses a thorough grooming and check as well as continuing our riding and loose schooling sessions but the possibility of further trouble between our family and the neighbors was blighting the thought. I pushed the worry to the back of my mind when Jason arrived early on Saturday morning, determined that I was going to enjoy the day. We had a lot of fun in the ring, especially when Jason decided Maple might like to join in a few little exercises. The elderly pony didn't look impressed when Jason led her into the ring and when he released her lead rope she merely stood where she was and blinked at him.

"Walk on, Maple," he said encouragingly but she was having none of it.

"You don't think she's deaf, do you?" Jason enquired anxiously.

I didn't say anything, but put a handful of corn into a feed bowl and shook it. Maple's ears pricked forward immediately and she walked briskly toward the sound.

"Ah!" Jason was encouraged. "That's it, walk on!"

With a lot of patience he managed to get her to do a full circuit, keeping neatly in the desired track, but you could see Maple still didn't have her heart in it.

"Maybe she'd like a game," Jason looked around him hopefully. "I could try building a very small obstacle course – she might like that."

He spent ages constructing one out of poles and straw bales till he became aware I was bent over trying not to laugh.

"What's so funny?" He turned to see what I was looking at.

The old pony, after pawing the ground in several different places till she found one she liked, had lowered herself with a grunt of satisfaction and was now rolling, first one way, and then the other.

"She's making up her own games!" Jason laughed as he walked toward her.

With a mighty heave the little bay managed her first complete roll, small hooves waving happily in the air. Jason, now very close, was covered in the soft sand mixture which clung to his hair, eyebrows and clothes.

"It's up my nose as well," he gasped and choked and Maple, quite concerned, pushed her blunt little head against him.

Her own rough black mane was full of sand and the carefully groomed coat wore a liberal dusting too.

"I am not amused," Jason told her sternly, scratching her under her chin, which she just adored.

"I guess we'd better have to re-think Maple's training," I said, still laughing. "Maybe she's just too old to start learning new stuff."

"You think?" Jason shook some of the sand out of his hair. "Do you think that applies to Pearl as well?"

"Probably. As far as I know Dad's never loose schooled her but we can always try."

Pearl, to my surprise, was very cooperative and absolutely adored jumping the little course.

"It must be so much nicer for her to move without a big lump like me on her back spoiling everything," Jason praised the gray mare after her success.

"You're not a lump. You're already riding well, but yeah, you only have to watch a horse galloping around his field to see his natural grace. Even a first class rider can't reproduce that," I pulled the leathers down on Pearl's saddle. "OK, now that she's beautifully warmed up and raring to go you can have your lesson."

It was a brilliant day and, to my delight, completely unmarred by any trouble. The whole weekend passed in a glorious mix of riding and chilling with Jason and the horses and, as the next week continued in the same peaceful way, I rashly thought that our problems were well and truly behind us. Do you know what – I couldn't have been more wrong!

CHAPTER SEVEN

The next time trouble happened was on the following Friday night. Jason had come over after school as usual, gone through his whole routine of chores and riding lesson followed by more chores, and was re-aligning the bolt on Logan's stable door when Mom called from the kitchen that my food was ready.

"You go on in," Jason muttered through a mouthful of nails. "I'll finish this and see you in the morning, if that's OK."

"You know it is," I put down a massive hammer I'd been waving ineffectually around. "See you."

"Has Jason gone?" Mom put one of her yummy casseroles on the table.

"No, he's repairing one of the doors," I washed my hands. "But don't worry, he'll put the tools away before he leaves."

She looked out of the window. "He's always working."

"I told you he was a gem," Dad sat down at the table. "You don't want to listen to Craig. His exams have him so uptight he can't see the good in anyone or anything at the moment."

"I think you're right," she opened the back door again and called, "Jason, would you like a bite to eat when you're through with that?"

I couldn't see his face but I imagined that great smile spreading over it. "Um, yeah, thanks, if it's no trouble."

I was in heaven, and super flattered when he showed no sign of wanting to leave after we'd finished eating. In fact he seemed to be enjoying himself as much as I was. The light had completely faded from the long summer evening before he carefully put the cat, who'd made herself comfortable in his lap, onto the floor.

"I'd better go. I didn't realize it was so late."

"I'll lean over the fence and check the horses," I got up too. "Craig's at a friend's house, so I don't know if he'll remember when he gets back."

The outside lights picked up the horses' outlines immediately, and I made Jason laugh by saying, "One, two, three, four, times four – yup, all legs present and accounted for!"

"You have to make sure one hasn't dropped off, right?" He gave my hand a brief squeeze. "They all look very contented, I'm happy to see. I'll look forward to seeing all eighteen gorgeous limbs in the morning."

"Eighteen?"

"Mm, I always make sure I check yours out as well."

I pretended to bash him on his cheek and watched him disappear into the shadows at the end of the driveway. Feeling relaxed and very happy, I spent a minute or two more gazing at the horses before blowing them a last goodnight kiss and turning back to the house. The evening sky was spread like a warm, soft blanket dusted with stars, wrapping itself around my peaceful world and the only sound – was an almighty crash as Jason's bike slammed into the wall behind me.

"You're not going anywhere!" Craig's voice was loud, harsh and furious. "Get into the house and explain just what you're doing out here at this time of night!"

I ran to them and tried to wrest my brother's grip from Jason's arm. "It's only about half past ten and he's just leaving after having supper with us. For heaven's sake, what is your *problem?* Let him go, let him go right now!"

Craig released his grip, shoving Jason roughly against me. "Well, he's found a really nice way of showing his thanks."

"What's going on?" Dad ran out to join us. "Craig?"

"I found this," he derisively jerked his thumb at Jason. "Holding *this*." He held up a can of spray paint.

"What?" Dad look bewildered. "I don't see –"

"No, but you will. Go and have a look at Bryan Edwards' place. Oh, he locks the gates at night now but he won't be happy when he opens them in the morning."

"Your son thinks I've been spraying graffiti on your neighbor's wall," Jason's eyes were hooded but I could see they held a glint of raw rage. "I've been trying to tell him –"

"You were holding the can!" Craig rattled it. "It's empty now, you made sure of that."

"I picked it up at the end of your driveway. It was right in the middle. My bike light shone on it."

"Oh yeah?" Craig stuck his jaw out aggressively. "That was convenient. So then what did you do? Test it out on our neighbor's wall?"

"Why?" I jabbed my brother hard in the chest. "Why would Jason do that?"

"Because he's a trouble-maker, a vandal, a hooligan,

take your pick. And don't give me all that logic about him not having a reason, because hooligans like him don't *need* a reason. I knew right from the start that he was the destructive kind, but you two let him con his way into free riding, free meals –"

"That's enough!" Dad's voice scared me. He never sounds like that. "Craig, I know you're under a lot of pressure but there's no excuse for a disgraceful display like this. I made you apologize to Jason a few weeks ago and I insist you do so again tonight."

"No way! Oh I can see he wouldn't do anything to harm the horses but everything else *must* be his doing. That day Buster got dumped inside Brad Tomas's garden – it had to have been done by someone who *knows* my dog – Buster wouldn't let a stranger get anywhere near him."

"But –" Dad shook his head. "We agreed that must have been an accident."

"I only said that to stop Brad Tomas's moaning. It doesn't make sense for Buster to have run all the way along the lane and forced his way through a hedge and fence, so who's the most likely person to have picked him up from here?"

"I didn't touch your dog." Two spots of color burned on Jason's cheekbones. "But don't worry, I don't expect you to apologize. You weren't sorry when you said it the first time and nothing's changed – you still think I'm some kind of lowlife."

"You got that right," Craig sneered threateningly and I flew at him.

"You total moron, Craig – stop taking your bad temper

84

out on Jason! It isn't his fault you're too thick to pass your stupid exams."

"Hey!" He grabbed my wrist. "If we're dishing dirt, Gemma, how about the fact that your boyfriend's only here for the freebies he can scrounge – don't kid yourself that it's you he likes!"

I lashed out with my feet and Dad, looking alarmed and upset, waded in and separated us.

"For goodness' sake!" He gave us both a shake. "I'm ashamed of you both and I've got enough to worry about without breaking up your fights! Just calm down so we can inspect the damage to Bryan's wall."

I took a deep breath and turned to look at Jason but he and his bike were gone, having silently vanished into the dark. The three of us plodded across the lane and shone flashlights on the garish graffiti that now adorned Bryan Edwards' wall and gate. It wasn't the artistic sort or even rude slogans, just great streaks and swirls of red sprayed indiscriminately across brick and woodwork.

"He'll go crazy," Dad said with dismay. "Bryan will be completely demented by this."

"I'll go and see him first thing and offer to clean it," Craig said, trying to make amends.

"Good idea, since it was probably you who did it," I burst out.

"Me?" His eyes popped. "Why the heck should I –"

"Will you two stop it!" Dad hissed. "If I hear one more word from either of you you'll be grounded for a month."

"You can't ground me at my age!" Craig protested but Dad held up his hand for silence.

"Then try *acting* your age for once, will you. Go home, both of you. I can't take any more."

Subdued and miserable, we trailed back to the house and I went straight to bed, hoping I'd wake up in the morning and find it had all been a horrible dream. It wasn't of course, and I was shocked at how haggard Dad looked at breakfast.

"He couldn't sleep," Mom told me quietly. "He was too distressed imagining what Bryan will say when he finds out."

"I don't see why. The graffiti's got nothing to do with us," Craig said, surlier than ever. "I mean, *Jason's* not family, is he?"

I spun around, eyes blazing and he shook his head.

"All right, all right, we don't know for sure it was your boyfriend but whoever it was has nothing to do with us."

"But the empty can was in *our* driveway," Dad objected.

Craig shrugged. "You don't need to tell Bryan that."

"Of course we do," I said, thinking he was seriously losing it. "It would be dishonest not to."

"I'm glad at least *one* of our children has a sense of what's morally right," Dad said wearily.

"Mm," Mom wasn't so sure. "I'm with Craig actually, Ken. The vandal, whoever it was, probably just chucked the thing away and it happened to land on our premises, that's all."

"In the same way Bryan's uprooted plants found their way here?" Dad shook his head. "You don't really believe that."

"OK," Craig gloomily swallowed the last of his coffee and stood up. "I'll go over and offer to clean it up."

"I'll help," I said. I was still mad at him but I couldn't let him face an angry neighbor alone.

"We'll all go," Mom said, putting her hand on Dad's arm. "We stick together, right, Ken?"

He managed a small smile and the four of us set off pretty nervously, I must say, across the lane. The paint looked even worse in the early morning light and I could see Dad's hand shake slightly as he rang the bell. Bryan Edwards' initial reaction was predictably irate as he scurried along the length of wall and gate, tutting and groaning.

"And you say you discovered the empty canister on your driveway?"

"Jason Brown, Gemma's friend, found it as he left our house."

"And how do you see that?" Bryan peered over the top of his glasses. "I personally regard it as a deliberate attempt to implicate Green Acres."

"Do you?" Dad blinked in surprise. "I suppose it must be, but I really can't imagine why."

"My guess is somebody thinks it would be fun to start some sort of neighbors' feud," Bryan said shrewdly. "In which case they're going to be disappointed. You didn't need to tell me where you found the can and you certainly didn't need to come over to clean up this mess, so I'm most certainly not going to blame you."

"Thank you Bryan," Mom said and she moved forward and kissed his cheek. "You've just restored some of Ken's faith in humanity."

"Good," he pointed to the jar Dad was carrying. "I might take you up on your offer of using that paint removing solvent, though."

"We'll help," I said and rolled up my sleeves.

"No, no, your father and I will tackle this, that's if your offer still stands, Ken?"

"Of course, Bryan," my dad was looking so relieved I wanted to cry.

They ended up spending a pleasant working morning, drinking endless cups of tea brought to them by Mrs. Edwards and, as Dad said later, chatting more than they'd ever done.

"I think Bryan was feeling guilty he'd overreacted about the damage the horses did," Mom told me. "And he's not stupid – he realized right away the graffiti wasn't our fault."

"That's good," I said listlessly. "Jason hasn't phoned, I suppose?"

"No." She looked at me. "He's usually here by now, isn't he?"

"Yeah, and we were going to ride to the common this morning."

"Maybe he's sick." She looked worried. "Or are you thinking he's staying away because of what Craig said last night?"

"Well yeah, Craig was horrible."

"Then call Jason and tell him it wasn't you, me or Dad doing the accusing and that the rest of us are happy to have him here."

"OK, thanks, Mom," I tried his number but found his phone was switched off.

I drifted back to the yard and considered riding out on my own but for once in my life it didn't appeal to me without the company I'd been looking forward to. Craig's words had obviously wounded Jason deeply and if he wouldn't answer my calls I didn't see how I was going to put things right. I did some loose schooling and a little dressage but when lunchtime came and there was still no contact I felt sick with disappointment. I put Logan back into the field, but even his affectionate reunion with Khan didn't bring a smile to my face.

"Come on," Mom said briskly as she cleared the lunch dishes. "I'm going into Brigham and you're coming with me."

"No way. I hate shopping." Retail therapy just doesn't work for me.

"*I'm* hitting the shops. *You're* fixing with Jason," she said as she looked me over critically. "You've got to change out of your horsey stuff because of his sister's allergy so go and put something decent on."

I argued a little, but only half-heartedly and twenty minutes later we were in the car heading for the Brigham Road. As we passed Brad Tomas's house he was driving through the electronic gates that guarded it and when he saw us he inclined his head in a stiff little bow.

"Oh well," Mom said philosophically. "Reasonably friendly anyway – and there was no paint on his gates, was there?"

"No," I'd checked too. "It's just as well. I can't see him being as understanding as Bryan!"

I felt nervous and my insides were fluttering as I got out of the car in the town center.

"Call me if there's a problem," Mom's eyes were gleaming at the prospect of her shopping. "Otherwise just be back here in two hours, OK?"

"OK," I took a deep breath and started walking.

Jason lived near the park, I knew, and I found his street easily. It was a long terrace of houses with small front yards and his house, number 31, was about halfway down. I rang the bell and licked my lips shakily, feeling very unsure about the reception I was going to get. Jason opened the door and when I saw the wary, hostile expression in his eyes I knew this was going to be tricky.

"Hi," I said brightly. "I was just – uh – passing by so I thought I'd stop in and say hello."

He raised his eyebrows. "Oh yeah?"

"Yeah," I plunged on. "So – hello."

"Hello," his voice was surly and for a moment I thought he was just going to shut the door in my face.

"So," I wished I'd planned what to say. "Do you want to show me this park of yours?"

"Who is it, Jason?" a woman with the same dark eyes joined him.

"Mom, this is Gemma, who instead of riding her horse out in the countryside, wants a lovely walk to Brigham Park."

"Don't be snippy," his Mom said and gave him a shove. "And don't leave your friend on the doorstep. Come in, Gemma."

The house was small and very neat despite the wheelchair and other invalid equipment around.

"Where's your sister?" I looked around. "I thought she might like to come with us."

"Helen's having a bad day so she won't want to go out, but it was a kind thought," Jason's Mom bustled around the shining little kitchen. "Would you like something to drink?"

I looked at Jason and he said slowly, "Nah. We'll head off for the park."

"Good," she looked at him fondly. "You shouldn't be spending a lovely day like this hanging around the house. Go and sort out whatever's been bothering you."

He grunted and started moving toward the front door again.

"Goodbye Mrs. Brown, it was nice meeting you," I said politely and to my surprise she gave my arm a gentle squeeze.

"Likewise. I can see now why Jason's been so miserable this morning and I'm glad you two are getting back together."

I blushed a bit. She made it sound as though we'd had a lovers' quarrel or something, and quickly followed Jason out of the house. He was slouching along, hands in pockets, head down, looking moody and unapproachable. I tried a few more bright, cheery remarks about nothing in particular and got virtually no response so when we reached the square of grass bordered by a few straggling trees that obviously constituted Brigham Park, I stopped dead in front of him.

"Look, Jason, I'm sorry about what Craig said last night. *I* know it wasn't you who did the graffiti and so do my mom and dad. Craig's just nuts, but the rest of us aren't and we don't want you staying away."

He looked directly at me for the first time and there was a faint gleam of hope in his eyes. "I'm staying away because all I do is bring you trouble."

"No you don't. *Someone's* trying to cause us grief but it isn't you. Even Bryan Edwards realizes last night was a complete setup."

"That's good, but I don't like you thinking I'm coming along just for the freebies like Craig said," he swallowed painfully. "The riding and being with the horses is great and your folks being kind to me – I like all that, but I'm not scrounging."

"I know that," I said gently. "You more than pay for everything with all the work you do and – um – I like you being around anyway."

"Yeah?" The light in his eyes intensified. "That's how I feel too, but your brother –"

"Craig's a moron," I said dismissively, still not wanting to admit I was worried about my brother's motives. "He's having a brain drain lately and even Dad's totally fed up with him. Come on over later and we can still get that ride on the common. Pearl was disappointed not going out this morning and I'm sure Khan kept looking for you too."

"No!" His face was lit up by that fabulous grin.

"Definitely," I grinned back. "You'd be letting them both down if you don't turn up again."

"OK," he said, looking like a different person now. "What time?"

I looked at my watch. "Mom's picking me up at four so make it half past? Hey – isn't that Vinny over there?"

Away to our right was a children's play area of colored swings and slides and I could see three tall figures moving around it.

"Oh great," Jason groaned. "Look at him pushing Mac on that merry-go-round. They've been chased out of there lots of times for damaging stuff – they never learn."

As we watched, Rick looked up and spotted us,

nudging Vinny and pointing in our direction. I gritted my teeth and silently psyched myself up for their approach, not wanting to let Jason know they worried me.

"Come on," he said quietly and walked away. "You don't want to be mixing with that bunch."

I could hear Vinny yelling something as the muscle in Jason's jaw tightened, but he ignored it and we were soon out of sight and sound of the playground. We spent some time by the pond in the center of the park, watching people feeding the ducks and sailing toy boats and we talked and talked and *talked*. I was surprised when Jason told me it was 3:30 and we should be going.

"I'll go and get my bike and make sure Mom and Helen don't want anything, and then I'll go with you to the Mall."

"There's no need," I said. "I can find my way."

"Vinny might take it in his stupid head to follow you," he looked grim. "I must have been nuts to hang out with that guy. He's just bad news."

"Your mom will be pleased that you've stopped hanging out with him."

"Yeah, she wants me to have a life, and feels guilty most of her time is taken up with Helen. She never did like me being with Vinny so when I found you and the horses she was thrilled."

As promised he walked with me to the town center, pushing his bike and smiling a bit uncertainly when my Mom came trundling out to meet us, laden with purchases.

"I found a terrific place having a sale," she said and handed me some shopping bags. "There's a lovely pink top for you, Gemma."

"Pink!" I said in horror and Jason laughed.

"Are you coming back with us, Jason?" She was hunting for her keys. "I've got the station wagon so I can stow your bike in the back if you like."

"Oh great, thanks." He helped carry some of the packages back to the car park and we were soon driving back out of town.

Mom always slows right down when we reach our lane in case any horse riders are using it so, seeing the gates of Brad Tomas's place were open, we were able to have a good look inside. The man himself was emerging from the big garage alongside his house, carefully locking its double doors behind him. Mom waved cheerfully but this time instead of returning the greeting he shot us a look of startled horror and quickly pressed a button on the remote he was carrying. The tall, impenetrable looking gates slid shut immediately, blocking out our view and letting us know in no uncertain terms that our interest was more than unwelcome.

CHAPTER EIGHT

"Look at that!" Mom said crossly. "He took one look at us and slammed the gates shut! What *is* the matter with the man?"

"He probably spotted me," Jason said ruefully. "He doesn't like what he calls 'my type' spying on his property."

"We weren't spying," I objected. "Anyway, what is there to see? He's just a bad-tempered old grouch."

Dad, puttering happily around the garden with Scala, was pleased to see Jason, and Craig, to my relief, had gone out. I swiftly changed into my riding gear, though I kept on the top I'd been wearing because Jason had already mentioned I looked nice in it. We got Logan and Pearl ready in super-quick time and set off for the common, which was warm and glowing in the late afternoon sun. Jason's riding was coming along really well and he was also flatteringly impressed by the way Logan and I handled the few jumps we took along the way.

"You two look great together," he put his head to one side and regarded us solemnly. "As though you're sort of one entity."

"You couldn't say anything better than that." I beamed at him. "It's what every true rider is aiming for."

"I hope I can make it to that level," he said and patted Pearl fondly. "I'm sure going to try."

His attitude and natural affinity with horses made it a joy to teach him, in fact most of the time I forgot I was the teacher – I was having such a good time. Logan was full of energy and also enjoyed himself enormously, and even the stately Pearl danced across the springy turf like a two-year-old. Back in the paddock the two of them trotted eagerly to rejoin their friends and Jason was sure they were telling Khan and Maple all about the fun they'd had.

"Look at them," he pointed to where the two geldings stood nose to nose, breathing in each other's scent. "Logan's saying it's about time Khan spent a wonderful afternoon like he's just had."

"You're probably right," I shrugged. "It doesn't seem to be a priority for Craig though."

"Sorry to say it again, but your brother's a jerk," he said, giving me a sidelong glance.

"No he's not." It was all right for me to criticize Craig but I wasn't letting him do it. "Just because you two don't like each other –"

"OK, OK," his eyes had gone dark and moody. "Let's just stay off the subject, OK?"

I sighed inwardly, wishing things were easier but it was impossible to be gloomy watching a glorious sunset as the red disc in the sky slid below the rim of the earth while we lay on the grass close to the four horses.

"This is a little nicer than Brigham Park, wouldn't you say?" Jason had regained his good mood.

"Well, just a little," I agreed, stuffing grass down the neck of his T-shirt.

"Hey you!" He was careful not to disturb the ponies but still managed to grab my boot and remove it.

"Give it back!" Giggling, I hopped after him as he ran to the yard, stopping to have one last cuddle with Logan as I left.

"I'd better go," he said and handed me back my boot with a flourish. "It's getting dark; must be late."

"I've got burgers tonight," Mom called out. "Do you want a couple, Jason?"

The atmosphere in our kitchen was even more good-natured than usual, with Dad in a much more relaxed mood after his friendly day with Bryan.

"He's a nice guy, you know," he told us. "I mean, I always thought of him as a kind of odd, fussy little man but once you get to know him he's – well – very nice."

"Our graffiti artist did us a favor then," Mom smiled at him. "Even if that *wasn't* his intention. Instead of stirring things up it actually means you're on better terms with the neighbors than ever before."

We drank an orange juice toast to that and in fact were actually clinking glasses when yet again chaos erupted outside. With a blaring horn and a screech of tires a car pulled up, scattering gravel that rained on the window like hail stones. Its door slammed loudly and someone ran to the front door and hammered on it.

"Who the –?" Dad went pale.

"Come out!" It was Brad Tomas's voice. "I know you're in there with that young thug. Bring him out now before I call the police!"

"Thug? Does he mean me?" A dark flush spread across Jason's face.

97

"This time Mr. Tomas has gone too far," Dad jumped to his feet. "First he threatens to shoot our dog and now he's insulting our friends. I've had just about enough!"

"Let me deal with him," Mom said, quicker reaching the door. "You'll only get yourself in a tizzy."

"But –" he blundered behind her and I ran after him and grabbed his arm.

"Mom's right, you'll get too upset – we'll stay here till she's calmed the maniac down."

"I'm not hiding behind my wife," Dad caught up with her as she opened the front door.

Brad Tomas was on the step, his voice shaking with anger.

"Where is he?" He tried to peer inside the house but Dad moved to block his view.

"Good evening Mr. Tomas," Mom said sweetly. "Is this a social call?"

"Social? Oh very funny! I've come for that young vandal – or did he run back to Brigham once he'd played his nasty little trick?"

"We don't *have* vandals in this house," Dad shifted his bulky frame enough for me to get a glimpse of our neighbor's furious expression. "So if you can't speak civilly I suggest you remove yourself from our premises."

"Then you'd rather speak to the police, would you? Because I'm telling you that unless I get some answers I'm going to call them right now!"

"Perhaps if you'd calm down and tell us exactly what the problem is we could help?" Mom was holding onto Dad as if physically restraining him.

"I *am* calm." Brad's voice was at least three octaves higher than it should have been. "Considering I'm yet again the victim of this household's wanton law breaking. You can't deny it. I followed the trail of paint from my gate to this driveway."

"Paint?" Jason stepped forward. "Spray paint?"

"As if you didn't know," Brad curled his lip in an ugly sneer. "I knew as soon as I spotted you trying to see into my grounds today that there'd be trouble. You couldn't break in so you vented your anger by defacing my property."

"When? When did this happen?" Mom was the only one keeping her cool.

"Now, this evening, probably as soon as it got dark. I saw this lowlife in your car earlier and –"

"Please refrain from name calling," Mom said briskly. "You'll only have to apologize. This young man's name is Jason and *Jason* has been here, in full view of my family and me since we saw you this afternoon. There is absolutely no way he can be responsible for any damage to your house."

"Not the house, the gates," Brad mumbled, looking disconcerted. "Red paint sprayed all over them and a trail of leaking drips leading to your house – my car lights showed them clearly."

I saw the tense line of Dad's shoulders slump dejectedly.

"Then someone has deliberately tried to implicate us," Mom's voice was still amazingly calm. "Because I can assure you quite categorically, Mr. Tomas, that the culprit is not here."

"I suppose I must take your word," he shot Jason a venomous look. "Perhaps on this occasion *Jason* isn't the guilty party, but can you vouch for his friends? On a previous occasion at least three youths of his type illegally entered my grounds."

"Jason's here on his own," I put in quickly. "And as Mom says, the trail of paint has got to be a deliberate set up. No one's stupid enough to do that accidentally."

Brad Tomas made a curious noise which I took to be a scornful snort and turned on his heel. "Personally I think anyone stupid enough to indulge in mindless vandalism is capable of anything, but as it's hard to prove I shall not be calling the police. Be warned though – one more incident and I'll definitely have the law on you."

"An apology would be nice," Dad glared at his retreating back. "But I suppose that's too much to hope for, is it?"

Brad climbed into his car and glared back. "Far too much. Once again I'm not at all convinced of this family's innocence."

He slammed the door shut and efficiently reversed the big car up the drive.

"That man!" Mom said crossly. "I've a good mind to report *him* for harassment! Where are you going, Ken?"

Dad had grabbed his shoes and a flashlight. "I'm going to check out this so-called paint trail."

"I'll get my bike and come with you," Jason said. "I've got to go home anyway."

"And I have to check the horses," I walked with him. "Seeing as Craig's not around again."

It was another hour before my brother appeared and he didn't seem at all shocked to hear what had been going on.

"You didn't think the graffiti on Bryan Edwards' place was a one-time event, did you?" he said and slouched in a kitchen chair, scowling at us. "The fact that Bryan didn't blame us for it is all the more reason the vandals would try somewhere else."

"I don't follow your reasoning," Dad looked bewildered. "How would anyone *know* how Bryan reacted?"

"Maybe you'd better ask Gemma," he smiled nastily. "I bet she told her boyfriend all about it."

"Don't be stupid," I felt a great rush of anger. "You can't possibly think this is Jason's fault. Don't you listen to anything, Craig? He was right here with us when those gates were vandalized."

He shrugged. "Like Brad Tomas said, Vinny and the others weren't with you, were they?"

"You mean Jason got his pals to do the spray painting and then carefully leave a trail leading to this house?" Mom stared at him. "That doesn't make sense. What would Jason gain by doing that?"

"I didn't say there was any logic in it. Vandals don't *do* logic; they're only into destruction," Craig yawned. "And now that they've succeeded in winding Brad up again you can bet they'll keep going. Still, it's not my problem. I'm going to bed."

I was so mad at him I couldn't speak, especially when I saw the frown of worry that creased my dad's forehead. I knew he didn't go along with Craig's line of thinking but I also knew how much he dreaded any

101

more trouble. I told Jason all about it as soon as he arrived the next day.

"Vinny?" he dropped his eyes to stare moodily at the ground. "He's capable, I grant you that, but I swear it's not on my say-so and I can't think of any reason he'd want to agitate things between your family and neighbors."

"Maybe it's *you* he's trying to get at," I suggested, watching his long fingers move gently to scratch Khan's neck. "He might be mad that you've stopped hanging out with him and this is his way of getting back at you. If my parents believed you're behind the graffiti and the wrecking of Bryan's garden they'd throw you out, so maybe that's what he wants. "

"The garden!" His head came up and he looked directly at me. "It can't be Vinny! I swear to you we were miles away when those plants got dumped on your drive. Vinny, his brother, Mac, Rick and me – none of us could have done it."

"Oh yeah, I remember you saying," I stared at him. "So who could have – oh no, don't say Craig. It's like one of those recurring nightmares with you two – he blames you and you blame him."

"I know you don't want to hear it, but it seems to me Craig's been at the center of everything that's happened. He's always around at the time and –"

"He was out last night," I said stubbornly, still fighting hard to believe in my brother's innocence. "At a friend's place."

"Yeah, well maybe he got back earlier than he said," Jason said and watched my expression. "OK, sorry Gemma, I'll shut up. Look, do you want me to go and see

102

Vinny? I might be able to convince him to stop if it *does* have anything to do with him."

I looked at the grim set of his mouth and thought that I wouldn't like to be Vinny.

"No," I said slowly. "You're right – it *has* to be the same person who dug up the garden that's doing the graffiti. There just can't be two sets of people trying to cause us grief. Let's hope my Mom's right and that they've run out of ideas now."

We spent the morning working, but since it was all with and for the horses it was more fun than work. Craig had disappeared again, taking Buster with him as usual, so Jason did some more loose schooling with the neglected Khan. Again I was amazed at the rapport they'd developed, a closeness and affinity that already practically matched the relationship I had with Logan. To vary the format we tried doing the exercises in pairs, with Logan striding out at my shoulder while the "dark twosome," Jason and Khan, mirrored our movements. It was almost like a well-choreographed dance routine with Logan and me flowing in unison on one side of the ring while at the other end Jason and Khan echoed the serpentines, circles and diagonals we were performing.

"That was fantastic," I said, a big grin spread across my face when we met in the center. "Khan's doing absolutely everything you ask and he's loving it too!"

"He's a clever, clever boy," Jason crooned as he hugged the black horse. "How about trying something a little different now? I bet Khan would enjoy a little game playing."

"Do you mean Pony Club games?" I asked, slightly

103

doubtful. "We don't have much equipment and they all involve riding, don't they? I'm not sure, Craig –"

"Don't worry, I wouldn't dream of upsetting your brother," Jason's lips tightened for a moment. "I meant loose schooling games, like – I dunno – soccer maybe or an obstacle race."

"Soccer?" I burst out laughing. "You want to teach these horses to play soccer?"

"I think Khan would be up for it," he said, dead serious. "But if you're not into it, how about something simple – a kids' game like hide and seek maybe?"

"Go on, then," I said, still laughing. "I'll hold your horse while you hide."

To be honest, his first attempt wasn't a great success mainly because there wasn't really anywhere for Jason to conceal himself. I solemnly counted to twenty and then turned to look where he'd had gone. I could see him crouched behind the upright of a jump and when I let go of Khan's head collar the pony merely trotted over and blew happily into Jason's ear.

"Stop laughing, Gemma," he ordered sternly. "And we'll try again."

This time he covered himself completely with a stable rug belonging to Pearl and he huddled beneath it in the far corner of the ring. Khan looked around for a while then trotted to the fence and whinnied loudly.

"He's calling you," I said, starting to find the whole thing interesting. "He can't see you, so see what happens if he can hear you. Just quietly say his name."

"OK," his voice was muffled. "Come on Khan, here I am."

The black horse's ears twitched and he turned his head, intently surveying the ring.

"He's responding," I said excitedly. "Call him again."

Instead he gave a whistle, a low, clear note that hung in the air for several moments.

To my delight the pony trotted immediately in the right direction, his eyes eager.

"Look out or he'll walk on you!" I warned and Jason sat up and spoke gently to the approaching horse.

Khan lowered his head and nudged him again, then picked up a corner of the rug in his teeth and dragged it to one side, dropping it on the ground with an air of great satisfaction.

"Unbelievable!" I gave them a round of applause. "That was terrific!"

To my disappointment Logan wasn't as clever with the "hide and seek" act, seeming completely unconcerned when I disappeared under the rug and refusing point blank to search for me, but he was the undisputed star of the soccer match we played.

"Goal!" I sang out as the ball bounced between impromptu posts. "That's 4 – 0 to the Iron Team."

"Yeah well, the Black Team hasn't gotten the hang of coordinating hooves and feet," Jason was panting with exertion. "We'll have to practice a bit before we have a rematch."

Still laughing we walked the ponies to their stables to cool off while we did the same with a long drink in the kitchen.

"That sounded fun," Mom said, getting out the cookies. "I could hear you from in here."

"It got a little rowdy," I agreed. "Jason came up with some great new schooling techniques and he and Khan are becoming a real star partnership."

"Well isn't that nice?" Craig's voice was surly. "Considering the horse isn't *Jason's*, he's mine. I don't remember giving you permission to ride Khan and from now on I don't want you anywhere near him. You got that, *Jason*?"

CHAPTER NINE

In an instant Jason's expression changed from bright, open and happy to dark, shuttered and angry. "Yeah I got it. So you want the poor horse left bored out of his skull in his field all day, do you? You don't exactly bother with him yourself, but yeah, I'll stay away – why should I worry about Khan when his *owner* sure doesn't?"

Craig took a step toward him, fury in his eyes.

"You're losing control, Craig," Mom said sharply. "For goodness' sake start behaving properly!"

"Why should I?" Craig was at his most belligerent. "I *told* him not to ride. Why should I let the little creep do whatever he likes?"

"You stupid ape!" I practically spat it out. "Jason hasn't been riding your horse. Why don't you engage your brain before opening your big mouth?"

"What?" A vein in his temple throbbed as he turned to look at me. "I heard you say he'd been schooling Khan."

"I have," Jason put down his glass and pushed him out of the way. "But don't worry; I won't ever do it again."

Before I could stop him he'd snatched up his the bike he'd left leaning against the wall outside and pedaled furiously away.

"Now look what you've done!" I screamed at my

brother. "I only just persuaded him to come back and now you've chased him off again!"

Craig shrugged. "Good riddance. I meant what I said; I still don't want him around."

"Fine!" I stormed out of the house. "Next time you fall off Khan because you haven't bothered to teach him anything don't expect me to help. I hope you break your stupid neck doing it too!"

The last remark was pretty dumb and childish but I was bitterly upset and close to tears. I ran to Logan, leaning into his sweet-smelling warmth and hoped desperately I'd hear Jason return. Instead it was Craig who came into the yard and silently brushed Khan in the adjoining stable before silently taking him back to the field. I spent the rest of the day moping, constantly checking my phone for Jason's call. Several times I started to dial his number, but stopped myself, feeling that so far I'd made all the moves.

"Jason knows it's only Craig who doesn't want him around – I can't keep chasing after him to apologize," I said to myself. "Except, maybe now that he's been warned off about seeing Khan he won't want to be here any more."

It wasn't easy to deal with the thought that Jason's main reason for visiting Green Acres was to be with the black horse and that my company meant nothing to him at all. I really liked him and had started to think he felt the same way about me so the fact that he hadn't come back really hurt. I felt pretty sorry for myself, and by the time I went out to check the horses one last time that evening I was just about as low as you can get. It was another beautiful, still summer night, the air soft and fragrant, and the moonlight gleaming on the four contented ponies in their peaceful field. I leaned on the fence and watched them for a few minutes, wishing my life was as simple and carefree as theirs.

"They've got the right idea, haven't they?" Jason's face, as he appeared beside me, was no longer dark and moody. "You know, no quarrels, no misunderstandings."

"I don't know about that," I said coolly. "They fall out from time to time; odd little skirmishes, the occasional kick."

"But if Maple takes a swipe at Logan I bet he doesn't blame Pearl," he said sagely. "Or if Khan's being an idiot I don't suppose the others gang up on him."

"Is this your way of saying you're sorry you stormed off?" I asked bluntly. "Because if it is you should make it a little clearer."

"OK," he took a deep breath. "I'm sorry. Your brother obviously thinks I'm some sort of scum but I know you don't and you're the reason I come here. If you don't mind me being around I'd like to carry on like we were, without me touching Khan of course."

"Sure," I felt a huge surge of relief and some other warm and exciting emotion bouncing around my insides. "Though I can work on Craig if you want."

"No." He'd made up his mind. "I don't want to cause more hassle."

"OK," I said, still acting cool. I blew the horses a goodnight kiss and said casually, "See you tomorrow for your riding lesson then."

The week passed quickly in a whirl of school, then Jason's lessons plus another trip out on the common for him and Pearl, with Logan and me showing off our jumping prowess. We were doing really well again and Jason obviously enjoyed our time together. He studiously stayed away from Khan, and Craig, under Dad's strict instructions, equally studiously kept out of our way so it was nice and peaceful and again it seemed that life was settling down.

"I went to see Vinny," Jason told me. "And he denies having anything at all to do with the graffiti. I made it pretty clear he'd better not be lying."

"Right," I pictured the look on his dark face when he warned Vinny off and thought I wouldn't want to argue with him when he was in angry mood. "Oh, did I tell you Tessa's coming over this weekend?"

"Is she? She seems to visit pretty regularly – I thought you said she preferred the city."

"She does, but she's worried about Dad, my Mom says, so Sonny suggested they come over and try to cheer him up. That run-in with Brad Tomas upset my poor dad a lot and he's been on the phone to Tessa about it."

"Your dad seemed to handle it OK." Jason ran a brush through Pearl's tail. "He told Brad where to go and everything."

"Yeah, but he hates any dispute. He's got this deep-rooted thing, and he *really* hates the idea that someone's deliberately out to cause trouble for our family. Sonny told Tess they ought to come over again and try to calm things down."

"I see." He finished grooming and gave the gray mare a pat. "Do I have to stay out of the way while they're here?"

"Absolutely not," I said firmly. "Hey, you've done

110

a nice job with Pearl – she looks like she's starring in a soap ad – all gleaming white!"

"You know I thought you were nuts the first time you said you had two gray horses," Jason grinned at me. "I looked in the field and saw a brown one, a black one, a white one and a sort of pewter-colored one."

"Pewter!" I pretended to be insulted. "Logan doesn't look like pewter!"

"Yeah, yeah, I know, he's your own wonderful iron horse but I couldn't figure out why Pearl here is also called 'gray'. They couldn't be more different."

"That's just the wonderful world of horses," I laughed. "There's a whole new language to learn, isn't there?"

"And I want to know it all," he said fervently. "Is – is Khan OK, Gemma?"

"He's all right. I make as much fuss over him as I can and Craig spends some time with him in the morning before he goes to college. His exams finish this week so he says he'll really start putting in some work on the horse."

"I hope so." Jason kept his face carefully expressionless and I wished again that the two of them would try to get along.

Tessa and Sonny didn't arrive until quite late on Saturday.

"Sorry," my sister said as she bounced in and kissed everyone, including Jason, and I found myself wishing I was more like her (but only in certain ways). "We had to visit a client of Sonny's on the way and it took longer than he thought. Where's Craig?"

"He's out celebrating the end of exams," Mom said, going straight into family mode, making drinks and offering food, "but he promised he'd be back soon."

Sonny joined in much more than usual, being particularly attentive to Dad, I noticed, which I thought was nice of him. Jason was included in everything too so he was still with us when the hall clock struck ten.

"I'd better be going," he said and put down the playing cards he was holding. "Thanks for the food and games and stuff."

"You going already?" Sonny came into the cozy kitchen. "I wanted to beat you at that new game you showed us."

"Not tonight," Jason smiled politely at him. "See you in the morning, Gemma?"

"Sure," I picked up my flashlight. "I'll come with you."

Chatting away as usual we strolled a short way up the drive before I shone my flashlight into the field. The house lights illuminated a big swathe of grass as usual, but it was empty and the strong beam from the flashlight showed nothing either.

"Jason!" A cold fear gripped me. "Where are they?"

"Come on!" He leapt on his bike and sped out into the lane with me pounding behind him. "The gate's open!" I heard the alarm in his voice. "The padlock's been forced."

My heart was hammering so hard I thought it would burst. Jason's bike lights were on and he was scanning the ground outside the gate.

"These prints are fresh," he pointed down. "They're heading that way – toward the Brigham Road. I'm going after them – get your dad!"

Tears were already streaming down my face as I turned back to the house, and by the time I ran into the kitchen even my neck was wet.

112

"Gemma!" Dad leapt to his feet. "What is it?"

"The horses," Mom said instantly. "She'd only cry like that for the horses. Get your shoes on, Ken!"

"We need the car," I gasped, trying to control my sobs. "Jason's gone after them on his bike but I don't know if he can catch up with them."

"How did they get out?" Tessa was fumbling with head collars. "And when?"

"S- someone cut the padlock, it's definitely deliberate," I wiped my face savagely. "Come *on*, Dad!"

"I'm coming too," Tessa put her arm around me in a swift hug. "Sonny, you stay here with Mom and I'll call if we need more help."

The three of us piled into the car and Dad gunned it into life.

"I don't dare speed along the lane," he said as he reversed up the drive in record time, "in case the horses are wandering around."

"They might be in a garden like before," Tessa said hopefully, peering out of the window.

"I think everyone's been shutting their gates since last time." I'd managed to stop sobbing. "So there's nowhere for them to go."

The car's headlights cut through the black night, illuminating the quiet, empty lane. We were rounding the bend where I'd first seen Vinny when –

"What's going on?" Dad slammed on the brakes.

Just ahead a bike lay on the road, its wheels still spinning, and behind it two figures were struggling, the biggest one holding the other in a vicious-looking headlock.

113

"That's Craig!" Tessa jumped out of the car. "He must have gotten the guy who let the horses out!"

She ran toward them but I was quicker and I was yelling. "Let him go! That's Jason, you idiot!"

"I know that," Craig panted. "He tried to get past me but I could see he was up to something so I stopped him."

"He was trying to get the horses before they reached the main road," I screamed. "And now you've messed up again and they're all going to be killed!"

"What?" He released his grip on Jason's neck.

"I tried to tell him," Jason choked and gagged. "He just came out of nowhere and wouldn't listen."

"Get in, all of you," Dad ordered. "There isn't time to argue!"

Craig hadn't even shut the door when he took off, roaring past Brad Tomas's house.

"How far along here did you walk?" Dad's face was grim. "Surely they couldn't have gotten past you."

"I was just at Mike's place, back there," Craig said. "I came out of his gate and saw Jason flying toward me, looking like he was running away, so –"

"So you ruined everything as usual," I was icy calm now. "He might have reached them if you'd let him alone."

"There they are!" Tessa shouted. "I can see Maple, look!"

Ahead, the sturdy bay pony stood on the grass verge, her head turning this way and that, her long black tail swishing in agitation.

Tessa nearly fell out of the car reaching for her. "Maple! Come here, come on, sweetie. Oh Gem, Logan's behind her!"

The ice inside me melted and I sprang out, trying desperately to keep my voice calm. "Logan, come on baby, come and see me."

He whinnied and stepped toward me at once, and it wasn't until I buckled the strap on his head collar and buried my face in his neck that my heartbeat calmed enough for me to hear the roar of the traffic and see its lights flashing up ahead.

"Where's Pearl?" Dad leaned out of the drivers' seat and peered anxiously along the lane.

"She and Khan must be up there." Trembling, I pointed in the direction of the Brigham Road.

"Maybe they've stopped at the junction." Jason moved beside me. "If we lead these two quietly up there it might lure them back."

"I'll drive next to you so we can use the headlights," Dad said and ducked back into the car.

It was a strange, eerie procession picking its way along the last unlit stretch of the lane toward the menacing roar and harsh lights of the main road. The four of us walked as quickly as we could, the two ponies, now calmed by our presence, staying obediently in line with Tessa's and my shoulder. Dad's car crept along beside us and we peered desperately into the long avenue of light thrown out by its headlights. There was nothing, no welcome, wonderful vision of black or white and we had to face it – Pearl and Khan were no longer in the relative safety of the lane. I shut my eyes tight, terrified that when I opened them I'd see carnage on the busy dual highway – cars and trucks slewed across the road around the bodies of –

115

"Gemma!" Jason squeezed my arm. "There's Pearl!"

We'd now reached the junction and my eyes snapped open to see the rapid stream of traffic thundering past in both directions. But Jason was right – a few hundred yards away, on the very edge of the road, Pearl was moving on the narrow edging strip, head high with terror.

"She's limping!" Dad turned off the engine and grabbed a head collar. "She's hurt. I'll call her back."

"She won't hear you above this racket and she's ready to panic," Jason took the halter from him. "I can get there quicker than you."

He ran, fleet and sure-footed, dodging between the scrubby trees that formed a barrier beside the road. Pearl was still moving away from us, limping heavily now, and we could see Jason's tall figure approaching her rapidly.

"She's heard his voice," I said when I saw the gray mare's head turn in Jason's direction and magically, thankfully she stopped. With one smooth, gentle movement he was beside her, the rope safely around her neck, and I turned to look at Dad.

"He's got her!" The muscles in his jaw were working and I could see tears welling in his eyes.

Tessa leaned across Maple and patted his hand and I felt a big lump in my throat as I smiled shakily at them both. Jason quietly led the hobbling mare back along the narrow strip at the side of the road and when they reached the relative calm of the junction where we stood, he handed the rope to Dad.

"Did – did you see Khan?" Craig's voice was low.

Jason shook his head. "I could see a long way along the verge and he's not there."

"He could be anywhere," Tessa said. "If he's galloping he'd have left Pearl way behind."

Craig nodded, his face chalk white at the thought of his horse running panic-stricken amongst the traffic.

"I'm going to move Pearl a short way along the lane, then go and get the trailer to pick her up," Dad was running his hands over her legs. "She mustn't walk any further."

"Look!" Jason suddenly said. "That car's stopping."

A small sedan had pulled up and a woman leaned out of the passenger window.

"Have you lost one?" She pointed to the horses and we all babbled "yes" at once. "It's back there," she indicated behind her. "Stuck in the median. A few people have stopped."

Immediately I handed Logan's lead rope to Tessa. "Look after him. Go with Dad."

Jason and Craig were already running, my brother's bulkier frame slower than the athletic Jason. The highway curved slightly here and the strip of rough grass with its border of close-packed trees was wider. For a moment my heart lifted – if Khan had stayed at the side of the road there was a good chance he'd be OK – but then I rounded the bend and my hopes plummeted. Two rows of traffic still roared in both directions, separated by a band of tarmac and a low barrier, and there, on this inadequate safety shelf, shivered the black horse, sweat-covered and paralyzed with fear. A car had stopped near us and on the far side a truck driver had pulled in and was shouting and waving. Running faster than I ever have before I overtook Craig and reached the car just behind Jason.

"These people have called the police to ask them to

get here and stop the traffic," he shouted above the roar of engines. "They say he's been there for several minutes now, but you can see he could take off at any time."

As he spoke Khan moved suddenly with a jittery, sideways clatter, obviously desperate to plunge away and flee from the terrifying monster of a road.

"He's going! Khan, stop, stop!" Craig himself didn't stop, just kept on running toward his horse and I heard the screech of tires as a car driver slammed on his brakes.

I saw my brother go down, hitting the road hard and rolling over twice, before lying completely, utterly and horribly still.

CHAPTER TEN

By sheer good luck the impact threw him, not toward the center of the road where traffic continued to rush past, but into the comparative safety of the side, just in front of the stationary car. As I raced to him I heard the driver who'd notified the police calling urgently for an ambulance.

"Craig!" Trembling I knelt beside him, laying my hand gently on his face.

To my unspeakable relief his eyelids fluttered and he groaned softly, "Gemma! Get – get Khan for me."

"Don't either of you move," Jason was beside me. "The traffic's slowing a little – I'm on my way."

Before I could stop him he took off, sprinting through a gap between cars that had only fractionally lowered their speed. Craig struggled to turn and see him, clutching my hand in pain.

"He made it! He's reached the median!" I could hardly bear to look. "But Khan doesn't know he's there and he's panicking worse than ever."

The black horse was shaking with fear and I watched him plunging and weaving on the narrow strip between traffic lanes. The roar of engines was deafening but I knew Jason would be talking and a shred of hope caught my breath as Khan's ears flickered and his head turned toward the tall figure.

"He'll never be able to catch him – the horse will just take off!" Craig's voice cracked with fear and pain.

"Khan trusts Jason completely. He –" I shuddered as the horse took another clumsy, clattering step, but Jason was now close enough to reach out and touch him, moving smoothly and surely to stand beside him, his arm circling the sweat covered neck, soothing the poor, frightened horse with voice and hands.

The wail of sirens as a police car and ambulance roared toward us made Khan shake again but Jason steadied him and I heard Craig whisper, "Thank you Jason, thank you."

The police were highly efficient, swiftly bringing the traffic still rattling past to a temporary halt to give Jason a chance to move Khan off the terrifying central strip and across to the relative calm of the side where paramedics were dealing with my brother.

"They think Craig's broken his leg," I looked up into Jason's brave, beautiful face. "I'll have to go with him to the hospital."

"That's fine." He'd now fitted the exhausted horse with a head collar. "I'll take Khan home and check him over."

"Craig said – he said thank you," I smiled tearfully. "He's so grateful –"

"Just go," Jason smiled back as he gently led the black horse away.

The rest of the night passed in a horrible blur of hospital waiting rooms, and it wasn't until the next day when Craig was safely back home, bruised and battered, his leg in an impressive plaster cast, that any of us started talking about what happened.

"We have to face it," Dad said looking gray with worry. "We got off lightly. Craig's leg is broken and Pearl is very lame, but that's temporary. The truth is, they could both be dead, our son and all of our horses, *dead*. And someone did this to us, someone deliberately smashed open our gate and drove our beloved animals out toward that killer of a road."

We were all silent and I saw Mom, her face very white, slip her hand into Craig's as if to convince herself he was still with us.

He squeezed her fingers comfortingly and said, "They couldn't have known I'd make things worse, first by keeping Jason from chasing the horses and then by running headlong into a car. Pretty dumb for someone who does so much studying!"

"It's not funny," I said. I couldn't bear seeing my parents so distressed. "None of it was your fault anyway, Craig."

"Gemma's right." Jason looked directly at him. "Pearl and Khan were running scared, just bolting mindlessly; I wouldn't have been able to stop them in any case. As for the car thing – you only got knocked down because you were trying to save your horse. That's brave, not dumb."

"I should have thought before I ran," Craig winced a little. "I was lucky you were there, Jason and I'm – I'm sorry for the way I've treated you in the past."

"It's OK," Jason looked embarrassed. "To be honest I had some pretty negative thoughts about you but after last night – well –"

"Oh that's one good thing then," I smiled a bit shakily, feeling very, very glad I hadn't ever voiced my fear that Craig might be the one responsible for all the horrors.

"At least you two have sorted out your differences. Now we can really concentrate on finding out –"

"It's no good," Dad burst out. "I can't take any more. If someone around here hates us this much I think we should just go."

"Don't be silly, Dad," Tessa went over to hug him. "No one hates you. This is probably the work of some mindless morons who get a kick out of being destructive. You can't let them bully you out of the home you love."

He shook his head in defeat. "I've made my mind up. This place is worth a lot of money so we'll be able to get something smaller and still have plenty left for you and Sonny to enjoy that big wedding. And Craig – there'll also be cash to help start up a clinic of your own."

Sonny was the first to speak, his voice high with excitement, and then everyone joined in, in a great babble of noise, all talking at once. I alone stood back, feeling sick and shaken.

"Come on," Jason took my hand. "Let's go outside."

The horses were in their stables, resting quietly after the terrifying ordeal of the night before. Pearl, her off fore heavily bandaged, was fast asleep, stretched out on her cozy bed and snoring gently. Khan, physically unscathed except for a few scratches, was much less relaxed and he started nervously when we looked over his door.

"It's OK, Khan," Jason's voice had its usual calming effect. "You're safe now; we won't let anyone hurt you."

Even though they'd suffered less trauma, Logan and Maple looked tired and were dozing in the soft light, though my lovely boy gave me a soft whicker of greeting when he saw me.

"Oh Jason," I said, struggling not to cry. "If Dad sells what will happen to them? A smaller place means no room for our horses – it means – it means –"

"Shh, Gemma," he said and put both arms around me. "I'm sure your parents won't let the horses go. They're part of the family, you all love them. Give your dad some space, time to get over the shock."

"But you heard him," I sobbed. "He can't bear to think that someone around here hates us and he's right – they must. Only a person who feels real hatred would deliberately try to hurt us this way."

"Then we have to find out who it is," he said, still holding me close. "And stop them."

"How do we do that?" I dried my eyes and looked up at him. "We don't have a clue who they are – all I know is that no one in my family is guilty."

"I know that too," Jason said quickly. "And I'm sorry I thought bad stuff about your brother. He loves the horses – and there's no way your sister would put them in danger either. Anyway, she and her boyfriend weren't even here when most of the trouble happened."

"Then it's like I said, we don't have a clue!"

"I think we do," he looked grim. "Who is it who's so paranoid he can't even stand us looking inside his gates? Who complains about us every five minutes? Who'd obviously prefer it if we just weren't around?"

"Brad Tomas?" I stared at him and to my disappointment he released his hold and took a step away.

"Who else?"

I hesitated. "Vinny? Maybe he's madder at you than you realize."

"Vinny's a jerk but he's not bad enough to try and chase a horse to its death," he said bluntly. "But I'll check him out first if you want."

"OK. Dad's called the police, but I know I'd feel better if we were *doing* something. "I'll come with you."

I don't ride my bike that much – I prefer Logan obviously – but I managed to keep up with Jason pretty well on the way into Brigham. Going along our lane was fine but I found myself trembling at the thought of tackling the scary Brigham Road.

"It's OK," Jason said, seeming to know my every thought. "There's a bridge across the main road – we'll go over it and take the cycle track the other side."

"Good." I was greatly relieved to get away from the scene of last night's horror.

I didn't relish the idea of the town traffic either but Jason knew all the shortcuts and quiet back streets so it wasn't too bad. Vinny's house was on the other side of the park from Jason's, another narrow street of terraces where a group of ten-year olds was kicking a ball around. Jason hammered on one of the doors and waited.

"You looking for the Jamesons?" A cheeky-faced boy retrieved the ball from nearby.

"Yeah," Jason looked at him. "Well, just Vinny really."

"They're on vacation," the boy looked me over with interest. "Danny won some money and treated them all, my sister told me."

"When did they go?"

He shrugged. "A few days ago. They got a taxi to the airport. I saw them leave."

"Thanks," Jason turned away from the door.

"Well, that's that," I said hopelessly, "In a way I was hoping Vinny was responsible because then it wouldn't be directed at us – more –"

"Yeah, more my fault," he frowned. "I can't help thinking it must have *something* to do with me. Before I arrived at Green Acres your family never had any trouble."

"You mean you're sort of the opposite of a good luck charm?" I tried joking. "I don't think so."

"No," he was deadly serious. "There has to be a connection, and the only one I can think of is Brad Tomas."

"In what way?"

"Well, a few nights before we met I got into his grounds, didn't I? Then when Maple was lost I showed you how to get in there too. Maybe that's what's bugging Brad – we know he's completely paranoid about trespassers."

"OK," I said slowly. "But that doesn't explain why he'd start a hate campaign against my family. I mean – why not take it out on you?"

"He's not one hundred percent sure I'm one of the guys who fooled around that first time. I ran over and put the hat on his garden statue so maybe he got a glimpse of me, or maybe we were caught on security cameras, but it's not a positive ID. But he *knows*, definitely knows, you went inside the grounds to get Maple."

"So what if I did?" I got back on my bike. "It was pitch black in there so I couldn't see anything and I didn't do any damage so why would my being there make him hate me?"

"Even though it was dark I bet he thinks you *did* see

something," he rode beside me as we crossed the park. "It's made him desperate to get rid of you so he's trying to terrorize your family out of the area."

"No way." My bike wobbled as I turned to look at him.

"You think? Remember what he was like last Saturday," Jason said, more and more convinced he was right. "The minute he saw us looking at his house he slammed the gates shut so fast they nearly came off their hinges."

"Well, yeah," I agreed. "But I thought that was directed at you."

"That's what I'm saying – *I'm* the link," he seemed to find the logic irrefutable. "Brad Tomas has something to hide and he thinks you may have seen it, but there's also the fact that I spend all my time with you. Two reasons to make Green Acres the target, and he's doing everything he can to force you all to leave."

"Well maybe," I said, still not convinced. The whole thing sounded way too far-fetched. "It would be pretty difficult to prove though, wouldn't it?"

"Not if we come up with some evidence," Jason said, enthusiastic about the idea. "I could do a little spying – get into his grounds and –"

"No way!" I nearly fell off my bike turning around to glare at him. "He'd be straight down to our house to yell at Dad again. I'm hoping my parents will change their minds about selling once everything calms down. If you go breaking into Brad's place he'll hit the roof and another fight will just send my dad over the edge. You stay out of there, Jason Brown!"

He shot me one of those hooded, secretive glances that I hated and increased his speed, whizzing past me to ride down the lane. Angrily, I pedaled faster but didn't catch up till I reached our house. He'd gone straight to the stable yard and was gently stroking Khan's nose as the black horse nuzzled him over his door.

"Hi you two," Craig, shuffling on crutches, came out before I could say any more about Brad Tomas. "I want to ask Jason a favor – and you, of course Gem."

"Sure," we both said immediately.

"Um –" he leaned heavily on the crutches, "now that my exams are finished I honestly intended to spend more time with Khan, put in some schooling work, take him out more but –"

"It's OK," I put in quickly. "Our summer break starts this week – I'll be able to help."

"And Jason?" My brother looked directly at him. "Khan completely trusts you. I could see that last night, and I'd be grateful if you'd start riding him. I was an idiot not to let you before."

I saw the knuckles on Jason's long fingers go white as he gripped the edge of the stable door.

"You're sure? I'm a total novice, you know that right?"

Craig shook his head. "Gemma says you're a natural, and I think the way you and Khan are attuned – well, you're the person to bring out the best in him and he deserves that."

"What do you think of that, Khan?" I pulled the horse's ears gently. "Oh he's nodding, Jason; he says he thinks so too!"

Jason nodded too, obviously feeling too emotional to speak and Craig tactfully hobbled back into the house.

"We'll start tomorrow," I chattered away to give Jason time to take in the news. "A basic lesson in the ring, I think, so you can get the feel of him before we start trail riding. He's a lot more lively than Pearl and –"

"He's fantastic," Jason said huskily. "I'm – I'm –"

"Speechless?" I grinned at him. "Give me a hand with the stable chores then. You don't need to speak for that."

I was nearly as excited as he was at the prospect of his first ride on Khan so the moment he swung softly into the saddle could easily have been an anti-climax – but it wasn't. From the second the pair of them began their warm-up it was clear this was the perfect match. Khan, usually jittery and wound-up, was completely relaxed, responding to Jason's light, sure touch with a smooth alacrity I'd never seen before.

"You're doing better than *I* do on him," I said and watched approvingly as he allowed the horse to stretch his neck.

"I don't believe that for a minute but I have to say it feels great," Jason said, grinning from ear to ear. "I still can't believe I'm riding him."

"Don't let Pearl hear you," I joked. "She might be jealous."

"You don't think so, do you?" His face fell. "I spent a long time with her last night and your dad's in her stable now –"

"I'm kidding, she's fine. So how would you feel about a trip to the common?"

"Now?" His eyes gleamed. "Great."

As we left the yard Dad was talking to some workmen who'd just arrived.

"They're here to re-position the field gate," I told Jason. "Tessa organized it. The only access to the summer field will be from the yard so anyone trying to interfere with the gate will have to come right down the driveway and past the house."

"And if they do that the dogs will hear them," Jason nodded. "It's encouraging that your dad's doing that – does it mean he's changed his mind about leaving?"

I shook my head slowly. "He's still talking about selling but says it will take weeks and he wants to know the horses are safe for now."

"He doesn't want to go," Jason sounded more confident than I felt. "As long as nothing else happens –"

"That's what Tessa said. Before she and Sonny left she told me she thought Dad would be OK when things cooled down, but I've got a horrible feeling whoever's doing these things won't stop now."

"Then it's good we're both on vacation," Jason said firmly. "It means we'll be around to stop them doing anything."

I couldn't really see how. We could hardly mount a 24-hour patrol of Green Acres, but now wasn't the time to worry. Now was the time to enjoy the wonder of riding across the glorious sweep of open countryside spread before us. Warmed up from their short lesson, Khan and Logan were eager to quicken the pace and we cantered side by side along the broad swath of turf, reveling in the sheer joy of the feeling. Logan, responsive and enthusiastic as ever, flowed effortlessly along the trail, allowing me to keep a close eye on Khan's progress. His handsome black head was in line with my pony's iron-gray one and his outline was perfect with light forehand and engaged hindquarters.

There was no trace of the irritable head shaking and jogging he frequently indulged in with Craig and he seemed to be enjoying the outing nearly as much as his rider. Jason, I have to say, was in pure ecstasy, the light in his dark eyes glowing, his body language relaxed and happy. He seemed to pick up Khan's every mood, soothing the young horse when anything made him nervous and gaining complete obedience with his confident, sympathetic handling. We spent some time in the cool, dappled shade of a small wood on the far side of the common, where a narrow stream broadened into a gently moving pool. It's Logan's favorite spot apart from the galloping trail and he joyfully waded into the water, splashing the clear water in a diamond-bright shower around him. Khan followed more sedately, putting one cautious hoof in front of another as Jason quietly encouraged him forward.

"That's really good." I couldn't keep the amazement out of my voice. "We've never been able to get him in that deep."

"It feels wonderful," he said, his teeth shining in the fabulous grin. "Are you going to do any jumping?"

"Yes," I said and popped my clever pony over a log and up the bank. "It's a little too soon for you, though."

"Don't worry," he said, his expression blissful. "I'm not going to spoil things by rushing. I still can't believe

I'm here with you in this great place and I'm riding this amazing horse. It's – it's –"

"A dream come true?" I smiled at his enthusiasm and tried to push away the terrible thought that soon the dream could be snatched away – not only from Jason but from me too.

CHAPTER ELEVEN

Partly because of the way I felt, the atmosphere at home over the next few days was very tense. Tessa, who was spending the week with Sonny at some relatives of his in the North, was on the phone every night, trying to lift Dad out of the depressed, negative state of mind he was in.

"It's horrible," I told Jason as we rode back from our daily trail ride. "We've always been able to talk to our dad about anything, but none of us can get through to him this time."

"Do you know if he's definitely made his mind up to go?" Jason moved Khan to walk beside me.

I shook my head, the tears that were never far away prickling behind my eyelids. "I think so. Mom's torn in both directions. She doesn't want to leave but can't bear seeing Dad tormented this way. Sonny's tried to convince Dad there won't be any more trouble and Tessa told me she persuaded him not to put the house up for sale, at least till she can get here."

"That's good." Jason leaned forward and stroked Khan's neck. "I – uh – I don't suppose your sister's got any idea what will happen to the horses if the sale goes ahead?"

"Oh yeah," I tried to keep the bitterness from my voice. "Pearl and Maple will go to a horse retirement home and Khan will be sold."

"Sold," he repeated flatly. "I – oh don't cry, Gemma. What about Logan?"

"If I'm lucky I'll be able to keep him, but we'll have to lease stable space for him somewhere." Angrily I brushed the tears away. "Dad seems to think that'll be fine. I'll still get my riding, but the horses – our family of horses – will be split up forever."

"Your dad's trying to do his best," Jason said, struggling to keep his own emotions under control. "He's aiming to let you keep Logan and you'll be able visit the oldies, I guess."

"Yeah, *visit* – they won't be right there outside my window, will they?" I was really crying now. "And what about Khan? He's only started to settle since he got you and he might go somewhere where they don't understand him. He'll be frightened and confused and –"

"Don't, Gemma." Jason's mouth twisted. "I can't stand thinking about it. We've got to *do* something."

"What can we do?" I asked hopelessly. "It's nearly the weekend again and that's usually when the trouble starts."

In fact it was later that day, barely five days after the dreadful night Craig and Pearl had been injured, that once again a loud hammering on the front door sent Dad's fragile nerves jangling. It was, of course, Brad Tomas.

"Malicious damage!" He was practically screaming as he thrust some broken branches into Dad's hands. "My hedge, the same hedge your daughter admitted breaking through, has been deliberately hacked to pieces."

I wanted to scream back that I hadn't broken his stupid hedge in the first place, but one look at Dad's face, gray with stress and anxiety, told me there was no point.

Mom did her best, asking for proof that the damage had been caused by anyone from Green Acres, but she also seemed shaken and defeated. Brad left in a great bluster of threats and warnings and I rushed out to the field so I could cry on Logan's warm, comforting shoulder. Jason had disappeared, probably I thought, to hide his own emotion. He was better than me at disguising how he felt about the prospect of losing the horses, but I knew how deeply he cared. I wished he'd stayed, though, wished he was here with his strong arms tightly around me. Logan was wonderful, curving his beautiful iron gray neck to gently nuzzle my back, and Khan came over too, nudging me anxiously as I cried into his friend's shoulder. I stayed like that for a long time, curled between the two horses, my heart feeling as though it would literally break. From across the field I saw Dad go to the stable yard to check on the recuperating Pearl and Maple who was keeping her company. He then got into the car and drove away with Mom, a sight that produced a fresh crop of tears.

"I bet they're going into Brigham to see a real estate agent," I sobbed to the ponies. "Dad said he wouldn't be able to stand any more trouble and now that Brad Tomas has been agitated into complaining again – well, that's it! The house with your fields and stables will all be sold and we'll be split up. We've got to face it, boys, we might never have another ride on our beautiful common, ever –"

Khan, who'd been as sympathetic and cuddly as Logan, suddenly lifted his head and moved away from me.

"Don't go," I said, feeling desperately sorry for myself. "I need you."

He stood completely still, his ears flickering.

"What is it?" I took a step toward him and he turned his head briefly to look at me. "Come on Khan," I wanted to keep on cuddling.

Instead, the black horse moved further away, eagerly scanning the field.

"I wish Jason was here. He always seems to understand what's bothering you." I mopped my face and went after him but he was off again, trotting this time.

"Help me, Logan," I placed my left hand on my pony's wither and vaulted lightly onto his back. "Let's both follow him."

Khan was cantering now, mane and tail streaming, ears still flicking and Logan flowed effortlessly behind him. I grabbed a handful of mane and sat as still as I could, hoping the two horses weren't merely fooling around. I love riding bareback, but without even a head collar to help me steer this time I wasn't keen on having a flat out race across the big field. Khan, though, seemed to have a sense of purpose, aiming deliberately for the far corner of the paddock and as he neared the fence he gave a high-pitched call – a whinny of recognition.

"Someone must be in there." I eased my weight back as Logan dropped the pace. "I hope it's Jason."

I slid to the ground and stood on the lower rung of the fence, trying to peer into the dense growth of trees and brambles on the other side.

"Jason!" I called. "Is that you?"

There was only the sound of leaves rustling in the warm breeze and a short burst of bird song.

"There's no one in there," I told Khan, stroking his

neck in an effort to calm him. "You must be hearing things."

He dropped his nose into my palm for a moment, and then brought it up sharply as his big sensitive ears flickered violently.

"Was – was that a whistle?" I'd heard it too this time, very faint to my inferior ears but there was no mistaking the young horse's reaction.

"It's *got* to be Jason," I climbed swiftly over the fence and pushed my way through the scrubby trees and brambles.

It's only a small belt of woodland at the end of our field, an uninteresting patch that I'd never bothered visiting before, but I knew it bordered the lane so I fought my way through the undergrowth, looking all around me. Once more I heard the faint whistle and from behind me, in our own field, Khan made his answering call. Within a few minutes I'd gotten through, emerging into a quiet stretch of lane opposite the house where Craig's friend lived. I looked up and down the peaceful lane, listening intently. More countryside noises and, in the background, the muted roar of traffic passing by on the Brigham Road. Just ahead the lane curved out of sight and I walked quickly to check the next section out.

If it's deserted like this part, I'm giving up, I thought. *I'll go back to the field and try to calm Khan and just hope Jason shows up.*

Rounding the bend I was met by the sight of Brad Tomas's hedge, the road beside it littered with broken branches and leaves. The vandal had made a real mess, hacking great chunks out of it and I approached cautiously, not wanting to meet the irate Brad. Again the scene was

136

deserted – but just as I was about to turn away I heard the long, low whistle, louder now and obviously nearer. Taking a deep breath I ran, closely following the line of hedge, until I was outside the heavy, solid front gates. The destruction of the hedgerow seemed random, with long stretches untouched, but on the far side of the gate a big chunk had been hacked away. As I hesitated nervously beside it I heard the whistle again, still muffled but very, very close.

"Jason!" I breathed his name as I wriggled through the gap.

Ahead I could see a wall, not the house but an outbuilding of some kind, maybe a garage.

"Jason!" I said it louder this time, flattening myself against the wall as I crept toward a window. "Jason!" This time I called, quite loud and very desperate.

His face appeared at the window and the look he gave me made my already wobbly legs turn to complete mush.

"The door," he mouthed, pointing to his left. "I can't get out."

Running as fast as my jelly legs would allow I shot around the side of the building and my heart sank when I saw a truck parked hard against the double doors. There was no time to think it through, in fact I seemed to act on some kind of manic autopilot, wrenching open the cab door and climbing swiftly inside. There were no keys in the ignition but the truck was on a slope so it took only a few seconds to let out the hand brake and roll it far enough away from the garage doors to allow them to open. As I jumped down out of the cab Jason was already emerging from the building. He ran toward me and grabbed my hand.

"You're a superstar, Gemma, you're – you're –"

"Just run!" I gripped tight to his hand and we raced back through the gap in the hedge and didn't stop running until we'd rounded the bend in the lane.

"Through here." I veered into the belt of trees at the back of our field, and once we were safely out of sight I let go of his hand and turned to him. "What were you *doing* in there?"

"Spying," he said succinctly. "I got in and saw Brad and a couple of other guys so I hid in that garage."

"And they shut you in?"

"They didn't know I was there," he said ruefully. "They were shunting cars and stuff around and parked that truck so close I couldn't get out again. I didn't dare break a window or anything so I just tried with the whistle but I didn't think anyone would take any notice."

"Khan did," I told him how the horse had reacted. "He's probably still waiting by the fence for you to appear."

A spasm of emotion creased his face. "Really? He's worrying about me?"

"Oh yeah. But not *quite* as much as I am," I said and folded my arms. "How could you trespass in there after the way Brad reacted to the latest vandalism?"

"It's a set-up – exactly what I said! Brad is doing all these things to himself then blaming us. He knows your dad can't take any more and he thinks he's succeeded in driving you all away."

"You're not still working that theory?" I stared at him. "You *saw* that hedge – why would he do that to his own property?"

"I don't know exactly but it's definitely got something to do with us and – oh Gem, it has to do with Logan."

"What?"

"I heard him, I heard Brad Tomas say something cocky like, 'after today it won't matter,' and then one of the other guys muttered about it being a success. Brad said quite clearly, 'the iron horse – *my* iron horse'."

I felt sick, physically sick. "Logan!"

Again we ran, pushing and shoving through the dense, clawing strands of bramble and when we reached the fence my arms and hands were covered in tiny drops of blood from all the scratches.

I climbed clumsily onto the top rung. "Logan! Come here, baby!"

Khan, still pacing anxiously up and down, whinnied shrilly but it was my beautiful gray boy who reached me first.

"You're all right – you're still here!" I buried my face in his sweet smelling mane.

"Yeah, but look!" Jason was on top of the fence, one hand stroking the ecstatic Khan, the other pointing across the field.

A hooded figure was running, sprinting away from us, heading fast toward the gate. Again I didn't hesitate, plunging straight into action without any logical thought process. With one rapid movement I vaulted onto Logan's back and went after him. Behind me I heard Jason yell but I kept my pony going, urging him onwards with legs and seat. We were closing in, getting nearer and nearer and our quarry half turned, his features hidden by the gray hood of his sweatshirt. He veered away, ducking suddenly behind the field shelter and with only leg-aids as steering I couldn't turn Logan quickly enough to follow. By the time I'd managed to curve my pony in an arc, using just my legs and a light pressure on his neck with my hands, the runner was a good distance from us.

"He's going to get away." I groaned out loud, urging Logan faster across the grass.

We'd never have reached him in time, I knew that, and my heart leapt when I saw the black streak that was speedily running him down. Jason, novice rider Jason, was bravely galloping in pursuit on the young horse with no saddle or bridle, virtually no steering and definitely no brakes! Leaning forward, his dark head was almost merged into Khan's black mane, and I could imagine the hooded figure's terror as he looked over his shoulder to see the black, avenging fury bearing down on him. I wasn't sure at the time if Jason meant to grab him as he passed, but he made a sort of sideways lunge, hurtling through the air to hit the guy as he tried to get out of the way. The impact brought both of them down, and they rolled violently for several yards before Jason leapt to his feet. Khan, perfectly safe and unharmed, cantered smoothly to join Logan as we charged toward the two figures. The runner lay in a huddled heap, his hood still pulled over his head and as I slid to the ground I saw Jason bend and pull the gray fabric away. Cowering back, the guy on the ground raised his hand, palm outwards.

"OK, OK Jason, I give in."

Even before he spoke I'd seen the can of spray paint sticking out of his pocket and recognized the close-shaved head and arrogant features – Vinny.

CHAPTER TWELVE

I had seen Jason's face dark with anger before, but this time it looked almost black with rage.

"You –" Jason took a fistful of Vinny's sweatshirt and pulled him roughly to his feet. "It was *you* last Saturday! You drove these horses out onto the main road! I told you before what would happen if you hurt them, Vinny. I'm going to –"

"I didn't touch them," Vinny's arrogant sneer was firmly in place. "It must have been this guy –"

"Don't give me that," Jason snarled. "It was you all the time, messing with neighbor's gardens, spraying graffiti – you've even got a paint can on you!"

"Well yeah, I know," Vinny, clearly alarmed by the fury in his voice, was looking less cocky by the minute. "OK, I did the painting the other week but not the horse stuff. I only got back from vacation last night – I wasn't even in the country last Saturday."

"I think that's true." Much as I hated the creep I didn't want Jason tearing him apart. "Calm down, Jason, and let's hear what your friend has to say."

"Friend! No way! Come on, you scum – start talking and make it good or I'll –"

"I told you," Vinny had stopped struggling. "There's a guy – he's been paying me to do this stuff. Like I said, I wasn't here this weekend so he must have let the horses out."

"Someone gave you money to vandalize neighboring property? Who? And why?" I looked at him in disgust.

He shook his head. "Don't know. I got a phone call saying I could earn good money for doing it. This guy said he'd leave some paint and the cash for me to collect at Brigham Park. I thought it was a joke but I checked it out for a laugh. All I had to do was come down here, decorate the wall and gate across the road and dump the empty can on your driveway. It was money for nothing – I'd have been crazy to turn it down."

"That was after the horses were let out the first time and after the plants were dug up," I said. "It doesn't make sense."

"You think he's lying?" Jason tightened his grip on the sweatshirt and swung Vinny off his feet.

"I'm not, I'm not!" The aggressive Vinny I'd always found pretty scary had vanished and now, frightened of Jason as he was, he looked almost pathetic. "I don't know about any plants and we never meant to hurt the horses that night. We were just getting back at old misery-guts across the road."

"Bryan?" Jason shook him so hard his teeth rattled. "You let the horses out to get at Bryan Edwards?"

"Yeah, remember he chased us off that night, moaning because he didn't like us hanging around? Well, later on Mac noticed the lock wasn't shut on this field and the big white horse was hanging its head over the gate. We thought it would be funny to put the horse in the moaner's yard, thought it would serve him right, so we

just opened the gate. Rick had some candy and the white
one followed him to get at them. Then two others came
running after the first one and they went in too. We didn't
hurt them or anything – we just wanted to get him back
and have some fun."

"And you didn't care what happened to our horses?"
I said furiously. "Especially poor little Maple who went
wandering up the lane on her own."

"We didn't know there was another one," he whined.

"I was with you that night – I remember Bryan
Edwards complaining, but –" Jason tightened his grip
again, "I went off to look for Danny – is that when you
did it?"

"Yeah," Vinny was nearly choking under the pressure
from Jason's fist. "But we didn't mean to hurt the horses
and apart from that first time all I've done is the two
rounds of graffiti and the hedge, honest."

"So the other stuff – digging up the plants, putting
Buster inside Brad Tomas's grounds and the terrible one
last Saturday – they're all gifts of this mystery man of
yours, are they?" I looked at him. "So who is he?"

"Brad Tomas," Jason said at once. "It has to be. He's
been planning something to do with Logan and it was all
part of his campaign."

"I've been thinking about that," I said slowly. "And
what you heard doesn't make sense – not in the way
you're thinking, anyway."

"The iron horse?" Jason wasn't releasing his hold on
Vinny. "I definitely heard him say that."

"Well OK, but that's not the way most people would
describe Logan. A horse person would say Andalucian

or the iron *gray* horse – only you and I call my pony the iron horse and Brad couldn't possibly know that."

He stared at me, absentmindedly lowering Vinny to the ground. "What else could it mean? The man's totally nuts, paranoid about something – only *he* would pay a lowlife like this to cause trouble."

"I can identify him," Vinny offered. "Honest, Jase, I wouldn't have gotten involved if I'd known what a psycho he was. It was just for the money. I wasn't supposed to see him. He just arranged to leave the cash for me to collect, but I was curious so I went to the park early and hid. I got a good look at the guy who left it, so if you show me this Brad Tomas I'll be able to tell you if it was him."

"Good enough," Jason started walking, dragging his captive with him.

"You're going to Brad's house?" I couldn't believe it. "He'll go ballistic! He'll – he'll –"

"He won't be able to do anything if Vinny can swear he's the man who'd been paying him," Jason was supremely confident. "You stay here, Gemma."

"Oh, sure!" I said crossly. "As if I could do that."

To my surprise the big gates at Brad's house were wide open and we could see a lot of activity going on. On the drive the sleek car was being polished while a fleet of smaller ones were having cases and boxes packed into them. Brad himself was talking animatedly nearby to two men and he looked up sharply as Jason, Vinny and I approached.

"Coming to the front door for a change?" He smiled nastily. "It's a bit late for that. Still, there's not much point in breaking in any more, is there?"

"Sorry, I don't know what you mean," I took a deep breath. "Jason and I have brought someone you might like to meet face to face. This is Vinny Jameson."

Brad looked into the pinched, weasely face. "What am I supposed to say? Is this another of your spying, vandal friends? He looks a lot like the idiot we caught on security camera hacking lumps out of my hedge so maybe I should just phone the police."

This wasn't exactly the reaction Jason had expected and he shook the gray sweatshirt fiercely. "This is the guy you paid to do your dirty work –"

"No he didn't," Vinny said, his voice dejected but still holding the ring of truth. "This isn't the man I saw in the park."

I felt my shoulders sag. "Vinny was paid to do some of the damage that's been happening. We thought –"

"That I was behind it? My only concern has been to keep you all out. Your continued attempts at trespassing have been very worrying, but quite frankly I don't care now. You're too late – it's just been confirmed – the Iron Horse has won – we're off to the winning ceremony this very minute."

"Iron Horse?" Jason gaped at him.

"The prototype engine I've been designing," Brad Tomas beamed proudly, looking almost human, and in my brain several things fell into place with a loud clunk.

I looked at him. "You've been working on something for a competition?"

"A Design Guild Engineering Award, very prestigious and top secret, of course. I chose this location for its proximity to a main highway and its privacy and

145

seclusion. Or at least that's what I thought till your family persisted in trying to force their way inside."

"Oh, but we didn't. It's all been a huge misunderstanding and I'm very sorry," I could see Jason looking at me as if I'd gone crazy. "There really is an explanation and we'll give it to you in detail when you come back from collecting your award."

"You mean he hasn't been trying to drive your family away?" Jason was still looking very tough.

"Of course I haven't," Brad brushed himself down. "I've merely been trying to stop you all from spying on my work. Now please remove yourselves and your – uh – prisoner so I can go and enjoy my hour of glory."

"Yes," I grabbed Jason's arm and tugged him away. "I hope the ceremony is – um – terrific and I'm truly glad your Iron Horse won."

"What are you *doing*?" Jason still had his vice-like grip on Vinny.

"Going home, back to Green Acres. I want to show Vinny someone there who I'm sure he'll recognize."

"Recognize? You mean the guy who left the money? The guy who injured the horses last week – the guy who's driven your dad into selling Green Acres? He's at *home*?"

"Come on," I was running hard.

Jason, impeded by the lumpish Vinny, was slower, and when he reached the kitchen he looked around almost fearfully.

"What's the matter?" I came back into the room.

"I thought – I thought – not *Craig*, Gemma, surely?"

"Oh no," I was shocked he could even consider that.

146

"He and Buster are asleep upstairs; he's not the one I want Vinny to see."

"Then who? Who else in this house could have wanted to torment your dad into selling?"

"The person who wanted money above everything else, the person who pretended to be so sympathetic about Dad's phobia when all the time he was using it to force him into selling – this person here."

From behind my back I brought out a photo and saw the light of recognition gleam immediately in the pale eyes.

"Yeah," Vinny said. "That's the guy who paid me."

Tessa's pretty face smiled out at us but it was to the smug features of the man beside her that Vinny was pointing.

"Sonny, "I said. "It was Sonny!"

❂ ❂ ❂ ❂ ❂

Dad, when we told him, was deeply shocked and Mom completely disbelieving.

"It can't be," she said flatly. "This is Tessa's fiancée you're talking about. He couldn't have done those terrible things."

"Then confront him," I challenged. "Bring him here and let Vinny see him. If he's still positive Sonny is the man who paid him –"

"You *are* positive, aren't you?" Jason tightened his grip again and Vinny twitched nervously.

"Yes, and I wouldn't have done it if I'd known what it was all about. I'll say that to his face too."

"You'd better call Tessa and get them here as soon as possible," Jason said, very much in command. "Once I

147

let this piece of scum go it'll be hard to get hold of him again. If he stays here till he'll identify Sonny in person."

"They're away, visiting," Mom objected. "We can't –"

"We have to *know*," Dad's voice was full of emotion. "And if Sonny *is* responsible then it's better that Tessa knows sooner rather than later."

"Tell them you need to see them urgently about the house sale," I suggested. "If they leave right away they can be here in a few hours."

Tessa, when she arrived, looked pale and anxious, running immediately into the kitchen and grabbing Dad's arm.

"Don't tell me you've sold Green Acres! Dad, you promised to wait and talk about this!"

"The house isn't sold," Dad said quietly. "We needed you here, Tessa – and you, Sonny."

I'd been watching intently and was sure I'd seen a flash of disappointment cross Sonny's smug face but he kept his cool. "Of course, Ken, I'll do anything, you know that."

"Or if you can't do it yourself, you'll pay someone else to do it," Jason's eyes were narrowed.

Again a flicker of something showed briefly but Sonny's smile was perfectly in place. "What do you mean?"

"That's him," Vinny stepped into view. "That's definitely the man I saw leave my payment and the spray paint at the park, and I recognize his voice from the telephone calls too."

There was a brief silence and then Sonny, his urbane cool only slightly dented, started to bluster. "Who is this piece of trash? He sounds to me like someone trying to shift the blame for his own crimes."

"We caught him in the horses' field. He was carrying a can of spray-paint," I said, not taking my eyes off Sonny's face.

"There you are, then. Caught red-handed – literally. You know he's guilty of the graffiti so it's obvious all the other dirty tricks are due to him too."

"Like last Saturday, you mean?" Tessa stepped forward and shook her fist in Vinny's face. "You – you – how can you stand there accusing my fiancée when it was *you* that chased our horses out to their possible death? You could have killed them all – and my brother too!"

"Except that Vinny wasn't even in the country last Saturday," I gently took hold of her clenched hand. "Tessa, it was Sonny."

"No!" The color drained from her face. "No! Tell them, Sonny, tell us all it's not true!"

"Of course it's not true," he looked straight at her.

"So you've never been to Brigham Park?" I asked, still holding tight to my sister's hand. "And you've certainly never left cans of red paint and a sum of money there?"

"Definitely not. This scum is lying and I'm deeply hurt you'd even consider his word against mine."

I could see doubt dawning on everyone's face and said softly. "It's not just your word, Sonny. Vinny might be crooked but he's not stupid. He thought he might need what you might call insurance so he took a photograph of you leaving the stuff. I've seen it – it's a very good shot. So are you still saying you've never, ever set foot in Brigham Park?"

"Sonny!" Tessa was so white I thought she might faint. "You paid this guy to play dangerous tricks you knew would make my dad crazy?"

Sonny was watching me, trying to work out if I was bluffing so I reached in my pocket and said, "I'll show Tessa the photo, OK?"

His bravado collapsed then and he sank down onto a chair. "You and I needed big money if we were going to have the perfect wedding and somewhere decent to live, Tessa. Selling Green Acres would have provided that, and once I realized your dad's fears meant he genuinely couldn't handle conflict with the neighbors, it made sense to use the fact to persuade him to leave."

"Persuade?" Tessa couldn't believe what she was hearing. "You call trying to kill our horses, not to mention my brother, *persuasion*?"

"I didn't mean it to get that heavy. How was I to know the stupid animals would panic and run so fast when I chased them?"

"But even seeing Pearl and Craig injured didn't stop you! As soon as that little worm over there came back from vacation you phoned and promised more money if he'd keep up the campaign!"

"Well yes, having gone nearly as far as getting Ken to put the house up for sale I had to keep going. I got Vinny's number when I investigated the boys' background for Craig, and realized it would make sense to employ him. That way *I* would never be suspected because I wasn't around when the vandalism took place. This time we were hundreds of miles away so I told Vinny to do some damage at the Tomas place and also do some more – uh – graffiti."

"You ordered him to spray paint Khan and Logan," Tessa said, nearly crying.

Sonny shrugged, with a brief return to his old insolent manner. "Gemma was being a nuisance, nagging her parents to stay, so I figured if she thought her precious horses were being threatened she might shut up."

Tessa turned away then, tears pouring down her face, while I felt sick and Craig and Jason looked positively murderous, but it was our lovely calm, peace-loving Mom who actually responded. She'd been preparing a casserole, a great big pot of it, and when Sonny said that she quietly picked it up and slammed it upside down over his head. There was a terrific thump as it landed and he reeled back, falling off his chair as he choked and gasped at the flood of liquid and vegetables pouring into his nose and mouth. He lay on the kitchen floor, with bits of carrot and onion sticking to his carefully brushed hair and a trail of lentils sliding messily down his face.

✿ ✿ ✿ ✿ ✿

"I loved that part." It was the next day and I was lying on the grass with Jason in our favorite spot – the horses' paddock. "Mom made Sonny look like a complete jerk – fantastic!"

"It *was* good," Jason leaned up and gently touched Khan's inquisitive nose. "You'd have enjoyed it too boys, though I still think he got off lightly."

"Not really." Now everything was settled I was feeling generous. "He's lost Tessa, the fancy wedding he wanted, and he'll never be part of the best family in the world."

"Listen to you!" Jason mocked, but his eyes shone as he looked at me. "I still think you were totally clever,

151

working out who the mystery man was – and as for that bit about Vinny taking a photo –!"

"That was just desperation," I admitted. "It was just Vinny's word against Sonny's, and Sonny's such an slimy creep I was scared he'd bluff his way out of it."

"I still don't know how you worked out who it was, though."

"When Vinny admitted letting the horses out the first time and doing the graffiti, I realized Sonny was staying here when all the other things happened. I know I got mad when you suggested the trouble-maker was a member of our family but it actually made sense as far as motive went."

"So I was right!" he said and started to tickle me.

The horses looked down at us indulgently as I squirmed and giggled and when I could speak again I got up and hugged them both. "Not really. Sonny never was and never will be *family*."

"What does your sister think about that?"

"She'll be OK. She wasn't anywhere near as big on the idea of getting married as Sonny was, so once she's over the shock of finding out what he's really like, I bet she'll be glad it's over."

"Your dad looks ten years younger already," Jason sat up. "There he is – and he's bringing Pearl and Maple out of the yard."

"Craig says Pearl can have a quiet hour or two out here today. Let's go and meet them."

We walked over to the new gate, followed of course by Logan and Khan. Dad smiled as the younger horses greeted the two old ladies with delight. Then we all stood and watched them settle down together. It was a wonderful, perfect scene and I felt a great wave of emotion sweep over me at the thought of us so nearly losing it.

Dad put his arm around me and said softly, "Well done, you two. If it wasn't for you and Jason –"

I smiled at him and said shakily, "The horses helped too. Logan and Khan were fantastic, weren't they Jason?"

He grinned, his face glowing as he watched our happy family of horses. "Yeah, it's not just Brad Tomas who can celebrate having the best Iron Horse in the world!"